"*The Last Panther* is poignant and lush—steeped in the mystical, while set in a future snared by devastation. Mitchell offers readers a spirited young heroine caught between two very different worlds. Kiri's story stuck with me long after I reached the end of the book."

—Ingrid Law, Newbery Honor–winning author of *Savvy*

"This is a book whose every piece is beautiful and fascinating. As the last piece slides into place, readers will step back and see a portrait of a richly imagined (and imperiled) world that will forever change the way we look at our own."

—Eliot Schrefer, two-time National Book Award Finalist, author of *Threatened* and *Endangered*

"A boldly original, profoundly wise, deeply moving book. It's a rare gift to any reader, as well as to our planet."

—T. A. Barron, author of the Merlin Saga

"*The Last Panther* has the timeless feel of a classic, yet with a timely message woven into its tapestry of myth and quest. I will be urging everyone I know to read this book. Not only is it the essential story of our time—and perhaps our future— but it's also a moving and tender tale of love, connection, and community."

—Laura Resau, Américas Award–winning author of *Star in the Forest* and *The Lightning Queen*

# THE
# LAST
# PANTHER

## Todd Mitchell

Delacorte Press

Text copyright © 2017 by Todd Mitchell
Jacket art copyright © 2017 by Erin McGuire

All rights reserved. Published in the United States by Delacorte Press, an imprint of Random House Children's Books, a division of Penguin Random House LLC, New York.

Delacorte Press is a registered trademark and the colophon is a trademark of Penguin Random House LLC.

Visit us on the Web! randomhousekids.com

Educators and librarians, for a variety of teaching tools, visit us at RHTeachersLibrarians.com

*Library of Congress Cataloging-in-Publication Data*
Names: Mitchell, Todd, author.
Title: The last panther / Todd Mitchell.
Description: First edition. | New York : Delacorte Press, [2017] |
Summary: "An eleven-year-old girl discovers a family of panthers that were thought to be extinct. But when others find out they are alive, too, she must risk everything to save the species"— Provided by publisher.
Identifiers: LCCN 2016034306 | ISBN 978-0-399-55558-9 (hardback) |
ISBN 978-0-399-55560-2 (glb) | ISBN 978-0-399-55559-6 (el)
Subjects: | CYAC: Human-animal communication—Fiction. | Florida panther—Fiction. | Puma—Fiction. | Endangered species—Fiction. | BISAC: JUVENILE NONFICTION / Animals / Jungle Animals. | JUVENILE FICTION / Nature & the Natural World / General (see also headings under Animals). | JUVENILE NONFICTION / Social Issues / Self-Esteem & Self-Reliance.
Classification: LCC PZ7.M6955 Las 2017 | DDC [Fic]—dc23

The text of this book is set in 11.5-point Sabon.
Interior design by Trish Parcell

Printed in the United States of America
10 9 8 7 6 5 4 3 2 1
First Edition

*For Addison Story and Cailin Elizabeth.*
*May the secret heart of wonder always be there for you.*

*What is a species worth?*

# PART I

*Devi of the Water*

# –1–

# The Secret Heart of Wonder

The netters were pulling something to shore. Kiri couldn't see what they'd caught from where she stood on the beach with Paulo, but six or seven netters had waded into the surf to haul on the lines, so whatever the nets held, it must have been big.

"That looks like your da," said Kiri, pointing to the netter farthest from shore. He had black wavy hair like Paulo, and his red shirt was soaked with salt water. It clung to his darkly tanned arms as he tugged on the lines and called out orders to the others. His patched and weathered skiff bobbed in the waves beside him.

"It is my da," said Paulo.

"What's he got?"

Paulo cupped his sandy hands over his eyes and

squinted. Late-afternoon sunlight glared off the surf. "Beats me. Everyone's nets have been coming in empty lately."

Clearly Charro's net wasn't empty. "Come on," said Kiri. "Let's go see."

Paulo hesitated. "What about catching sand fleas?" He nodded to the trap they'd spent the better part of an hour digging on the beach. "Tide's almost in."

"The sand fleas will be here later. Whatever's in that net might not." Kiri hoisted her bag over her shoulder, fixing the strap so it wouldn't bite into her skin. The vials of seawater she'd collected made the bag heavy, but Kiri was used to carrying it. At eleven, she was small but strong, thanks to years of trekking to the beach every day to collect water samples for her da. Paulo often claimed he couldn't even lift the bag when it was full, although that probably had more to do with his laziness.

Snowflake, Kiri's rat, poked his head out of her hood to investigate what all the fuss was about. His whiskers tickled her neck as he climbed onto her shoulder and sniffed. "Sorry, Snowflake," said Kiri. "Nap time's over."

Paulo smirked at the little rat. "If you're not careful, the netters might try to catch him," he teased.

"Hush! You'll scare him," said Kiri. "Snowflake is a very sensitive creature."

"I'm serious. People in the village are getting so hungry, I bet they'd make rat stew. Come to think of it, that's not a bad idea. He looks delicious."

Kiri lifted the rat off her shoulder and scratched the

white star on his head. "Don't listen to him, Snowflake. Paulo's joking. He always jokes."

She set Snowflake back on her shoulder. He chittered at Paulo before returning to his hiding place in Kiri's hood. When she let her wild brown hair—"motherless hair," the women in the stilt village called it—tumble over her back, no one could even tell the little rat was there.

A shout from up the beach called Kiri's attention back to the netters. Fugees from the nearby stilt village had started to gather around them. Whatever Charro had caught, it wasn't coming in easily.

"It could just be a tire, or some other salvage," said Paulo, squinting into the sun.

"Think your da would need six netters to bring in a tire?"

"Good point."

Paulo finally left the sand-flea trap and joined Kiri. Together, they ran toward the crowd gathering on the beach. Snowflake bounced slightly in Kiri's hood, but he was used to holding on. He dug his tiny forepaws into her collar and stretched his hindquarters down so he wouldn't fly out.

"Paulo!" shouted Tae, Paulo's older brother, as they approached. "Get over here!"

Paulo didn't leave Kiri's side. She felt grateful to him for that. Ever since they were six and Kiri had wandered into the stilt village for the first time on her own, she and Paulo had been best friends.

Tae shouted to Paulo again, waving for him to come into the water and grab part of the net.

"I better go," said Paulo. "Tae will snap a line if I don't help."

Kiri nodded. She wished she could join the netters in the surf as well, but she knew she wouldn't be welcome. Only fugees with a catch share were allowed to pull in the nets.

Still, she felt called by more than curiosity to see what the netters had caught. And so she followed Paulo, ignoring people's grunts and complaints. When she finally made it through the crowd, what she saw made her heart kick.

At first it looked like a huge log bobbing in the surf, except it was wider than any log Kiri had ever seen—as wide as Charro's skiff, even, with a ridged shell-like back and a stout, tree-stump head. Enormous flippers swirled the waves as the creature tried to swim away, but it couldn't escape. The lines of the nets had tangled around its limbs, and they tightened with every pull. The creature's shiny black flippers, shell, and head were all dappled with white spots like the sky at midnight. Its odd teardrop-shaped body reminded Kiri of a giant sunflower seed, if sunflower seeds could swim and were bigger than four gators put together.

Paulo joined his brother in pulling the nets in, as if his skinny arms would make a difference. Kiri stuck close behind him, but she didn't grab the nets. Instead, she wished she could do the opposite and get everyone to let the creature go. No one would listen to her, though. What netter worth his salt would release such a catch?

She stepped farther into the water, not caring if her

shorts got wet or if jellies stung her legs. Snowflake prodded her back as he nuzzled deeper into her hood, avoiding the shouting voices and the spray of the surf. The little rat hated getting wet.

"Hup! Hup! Pull!" yelled Charro to the netters each time a wave surged. "Step back!" he shouted to villagers who pressed too close.

Kiri didn't step back. She felt as if the fishing nets and lines were wrapped around *her* limbs, tugging her closer to the creature emerging from the surf. Barnacles pocked the edge of its shell, and its wrinkled skin looked thick and ancient. It faced the waves, but on land its massive flippers were cumbersome and slow, flailing in the sand.

A big wave came in. Charro barked more commands and the netters heaved the creature farther up the beach. Then the water receded, and for the first time, Kiri saw its eyes. Framed by thick gray lids, its eyes were larger than her fists and a deep, entrancing blue. The creature lifted its tree-stump head and fixed its bottomless gaze on her.

Kiri's breath caught. She'd always had a way with animals. It was why she was good at catching things, and why, if one of the netters would take her out on a skiff, she knew she could find some fish and prove herself to the villagers. She always seemed to know where creatures wanted to be, in part because she tried to think like them, and in part because of a whispery sense she sometimes got that they were speaking to her. But what she felt now, as she peered into the creature's eyes, was more than any whisper.

Another wave broke and the netters heaved the giant

still farther up the beach. The creature opened its hard-lipped mouth, but it made no sound. No sound in the air, at least. In Kiri's chest, though, she felt something like the rumble of thunder and she heard the hurricane roar of wind through palm branches—a rising, primal call that made her body quiver and her pulse race.

The waves that had given them shipwrecks and storms, washing ashore countless dead fish, along with salvage they sold to the boat people, had now surrendered this. To Kiri it seemed as if the secret heart of wonder itself had been hauled from depths unknown and made to flop on land. With its wrinkled midnight skin and its stunning blue eyes, it appeared both old and new. Both familiar and strange. She had no name for it. This giant's tear. This ocean's seed. This earth's ancient, forgotten dream, suddenly remembered.

# —2—

# The Once-Were Creatures

At night, before Kiri slipped off to sleep, her da sometimes told her stories of the once-were creatures.

He spoke of ones with necks so long they could eat the leaves from the tops of trees, scraping them off branches with black tongues longer than her arm while teetering on stilt legs.

And he spoke of ones that stood bigger than houses, with python noses that could lift a boat, and curved teeth as big as oars. He said they traveled in herds, like an entire village of houses moving across a field.

He told her of enormous ice bears, with white fur and black skin. And hairy giants, three times the size of men, who could talk to people with their hands. And white sea beasts with spiral horns sharper than spears. And jeweled birds that could hover in place and suck the sweet from flowers. But her favorite once-were creatures were the blue waterlords who were longer than six skiffs in a row. Da told her stories of how they made waves with their fins and sang songs in trilling, mournful voices that lasted for days. Songs, he claimed, that were too complex for human ears to hear.

When she was younger, Kiri actually believed such wondrous creatures had existed. The only proof her da ever offered, though, were drawings in some of the rotting waller books he kept in plastic bags and wouldn't let her touch. And most of the faded drawings he showed her were of creatures that seemed too big or strange to be real. As she got older, Kiri asked others in the village about the once-were creatures. All the fugees who'd been places and knew something of the world laughed and shook their heads at her waller stories, until she finally came to believe that the once-were creatures were just mythical things.

Now, though, staring at the huge blue-eyed creature digging its flippers into the beach, she wasn't so sure. If something like this, that was as big and strange as any once-were creature her da had ever spoken of, could exist, then couldn't others exist as well? Other water giants, and flying jewels, and long-necked spotted horses on stilts?

Charro climbed onto the creature's ridged shell-like back and stood above the crowd as if he were standing on an overturned skiff. The creature raised its mighty head to shake him off, but it could barely move its bulk on land. It looked longingly at the receding waves, then lowered its head and closed its ponderous blue eyes, not struggling anymore.

"What is it?" asked one of the younger netters.

"I've never seen anything like it," said someone else. "It's amazing."

"It's salvage!" announced Charro. His round belly poked through his open shirt, making him look like an overgrown, boastful toddler. But his eyes were sharp, and his bronze skin had been scarred and toughened from many years of fishing. There was little resemblance between Paulo's skinny, goofy presence and his father's large, stern one.

"Salvage, that's all," continued Charro. "I spotted it out beyond the breakers and I claimed salvage rights to it then and there. Tarun heard me."

"That's true," said Tarun, a quiet netter whose words carried weight. "He did claim salvage rights."

"So it's mine," said Charro. "Tomorrow, I'm taking it to the boat people to trade."

Nessa, Paulo's favorite aunt, threw down the clumps of net she'd been holding and crossed her arms. "It's not salvage if it's alive, Charro. It's a catch, and we all helped pull it in. All of us here." She nodded to the other netters, many of whom were wet from the surf and had raised spots on their legs from jellyfish stings. "Which means it's part of the catch share, so we all get to decide what's done with it."

A few netters grunted in agreement. Nessa's expression was all angles and hard edges, with her straight black hair pulled back tightly from her face in a way that made the bones beneath her cheeks stand out.

Charro waited for the mutters to subside before he spoke. "Does this look like a fish to you, Nessa? Does it look like a fish to any of you?" he added, addressing the crowd. "No? That's because it's not. It's salvage."

The netters who sided with Charro nodded. Still, some weren't persuaded and they took up Nessa's side of the argument. "It's a catch," said one. "You can't claim salvage rights to a catch."

Several women and elders joined the argument. With how scarce food had been lately, tempers were close to the surface, and soon the rumble of voices rose above the crash of waves.

Amid the clamor, Kiri noticed the old Witch Woman making her way through the crowd. She moved stiffly, her bad foot leaving sideways tracks in the sand. She was so slight that she was able to weave through gaps between arguing villagers without causing a fuss, until she stood in the open space near the creature's head. The creature lifted its round snout off the sand in response.

A hush spread through the crowd. Kiri wanted to shout a warning. Even though the creature was slow and cumbersome on land, all it had to do was open its massive jaws and snap once and it could break the Witch Woman in half. Others must have seen this danger as well, but no one spoke. No one dared. Everyone was stuck in the peculiar silence that descends the moment before disaster strikes.

Only, no disaster came. The Witch Woman stretched her knobby hand toward the creature until her fingers rested on its round snout, like a bird perching on a sinking ship. The huge creature gave her a long, weary look. Then it huffed out an enormous breath, blowing the Witch Woman's gray hair back. Still, she didn't move.

"It's no catch," she said in a driftwood voice. "It's no salvage, either."

"Then what is it?" asked Charro, glaring down at the Witch Woman from atop the creature's back.

"A portent," she said.

"A *what*?"

The Witch Woman ignored Charro, focusing instead on the netters, elders, and children gathered around her.

"It's a messenger," she said. "A *devi* sent by the Wise One."

Hushed murmurs spread through the crowd. Fugees rarely spoke of devi out loud. Some considered them gods, or fragments of gods that walked the earth. Others considered them demons. Or angels. Or both.

Once, after seeing Nessa make an offering to a devi before rowing out on a gray day, Kiri asked Paulo what devi were. "Devi are devi," he told her. "There's no other word for them." So all Kiri knew about devi was that some could be good, and some could be bad, but all were best respected.

"If it's a devi sent to bring us a message, then what's it saying?" asked Senek, a pale, sandy-haired netter whose face always looked red and sunburned. He often drank palm wine with Charro under his stilt house at the end of the day.

"Shhh . . . ," said Charro. He lowered himself to his hands and knees, still balancing on the creature's back. Then he leaned toward the creature's head and cupped his hand by his ear, making a big show of listening. "I hear it! It's saying . . . It's saying, *Charro, go to the boat people and trade me for new nets and a motor for your skiff.*"

This time the Witch Woman did look at Charro. She narrowed her eyes as if he were a rabid dog in the distance. "You'd do well to listen truly, *child.*"

Kiri's jaw dropped. She'd never heard anyone speak to Paulo's da that way. Charro sat on the council and was the best netter in the village. He brought in more of the catch share than anyone, and to hear him tell it, he'd kept half the village fed. He was loud and arrogant, but most of the things he said were true. Plus he had a temper worse than a hurricane, so no one ever crossed him.

Charro got down off the creature's back and surveyed the crowd. "I *am* listening," he said. "All I hear is a bunch of stories from an old woman who doesn't bring in a catch while the village goes hungry."

"Not everything speaks with words," replied the Witch Woman. "Open your eyes and tell me what you see."

Charro scowled and walked around the creature. "I see a new set of nets. A motor for my skiff. Maybe even a way to tug a couple of skiffs out to the deep currents where the fish must be so we can finally fill our nets and increase the catch share for all of us. So unless you like starving, old woman, you better shut your trap."

A few netters nodded in agreement, but others seemed doubtful. Kiri noticed many villagers in the crowd staring at the creature with wide-eyed amazement. No one knew what to do with it.

"I see a way to increase the catch share right now *and* fill our bellies," claimed Nessa. "You can't bring this whole thing to the boat people, Charro. And it would be wrong to let any of it go to waste. When there's a catch you have to share it. That's our way."

Charro stepped over the creature's massive front flippers to confront Nessa. He stood toe to toe with her, so close that his bronze belly nearly shoved her backward. "It's *not* a catch," he said. "It's salvage."

"It can't be salvage if it's alive."

"This isn't a fish, Nessa," said Charro. "Then again, I'm not surprised you don't know what fish look like, seeing as you haven't brought in a single catch worth sharing in over a month."

Nessa bristled and Kiri saw her hand drop to the knife at her belt. People around them stepped back, clearing a space. A few adults pulled Paulo and Tae back as well. A storm was brewing, and when it broke it might harm whatever stood in its way.

"I go out every day, same as you," said Nessa.

"You go out, but you don't bring much back."

"What are you suggesting?"

"Just that if you're catching something, we haven't seen

it. So either you don't know how to net, or you're not sharing what you get."

Kiri felt bad for Paulo. Nessa was his mother's sister and one of the few adults who looked after him. If his da and Nessa got in a fight, no matter what happened, it wouldn't end well for Paulo.

"You're the one who doesn't want to share his catch," accused Nessa.

Charro's eyes darkened. "For the last time, it's *not a catch*."

"Then what is it? You can't claim it's salvage if you don't know what it is."

The storm between them kept building. Someone had to do something before it was too late. Kiri looked for Elder Tomas, the council leader. Maybe he could keep Charro and Nessa from fighting, but Kiri didn't see his bald head and bushy gray beard in the crowd.

For Paulo's sake, Kiri tried to think of a way to stop the fight, only what could she do? None of the netters would listen to her. The strap of her bag hung heavy on her shoulder. Even though collecting seawater samples gave her a reason to come to the beach every day, it marked her as different. Fugees sometimes teased her when they saw her filling vials or taking the temperature of the waves and recording the numbers in a book for her da. "Is the ocean still blue? Is the water still salty?" they'd say, frowning at her actions. They tolerated her, but most thought of her as an outsider—a waller doing waller things—and if she

16

spoke out now, she might not be welcome in the village anymore.

"Perhaps the Witch Woman is right and it is a devi," said Tarun.

"It's not a devi," said Charro.

"How do *you* know?" countered Nessa. "You don't know what it is any more than we do."

"Perhaps we should let it go," said Tarun.

"What good would that do?" Charro scowled. "Look at it. It's old and injured. It's not going anywhere. To waste it would be wrong—that's one thing Nessa and I agree on."

"Then share the catch," said Nessa.

Charro spat and glared at her.

Kiri's gaze slid from Charro's angry face to the enormous creature beyond him. Most of the water on its ridged shell-like back had dried and its sand-encrusted eyes had closed. Without the sheen of wetness, its midnight-with-stars skin looked cracked and dull. A line of blood trickled from where the net had bit into its flipper.

Paulo squirmed free of the adult who'd grabbed him and edged between people to reach Kiri. "Your da!" he said. "Go get your da!"

"Why?" Kiri didn't see how her da could help. He barely ever came to the fugee village.

"If anyone knows what this creature is, it's him," said Paulo. "He can tell them if it's a fish or a devi or something else. He can settle this!"

The storm between Charro and Nessa had spread to

the crowd. Those who sided with Charro stood apart from those who sided with Nessa. More were on Charro's side, but Nessa was too stubborn, or too hungry, to give in.

"Please," said Paulo. "I'll tell them he's coming."

Kiri left the crowd and hurried toward the ghost forest. She paused at the base of one of the dunes, unslung her heavy bag, and tossed it onto the sand.

"Kiri's da, the waller man," shouted Paulo to the crowd, "he'll know what the creature is! He can tell you if it's salvage or a catch, or what to do with it. He'll know!"

A hush descended as Paulo's words sank in.

"She's going to get him right now," said Paulo. He looked over to where Kiri stood by the dunes and nodded to her. She nodded back, then set off at a run. Without the bag full of water samples, she felt light and swift as the wind. Her da *would* know. He could stop the fight and maybe even save the magnificent blue-eyed creature.

For once, Kiri thought, the people in the village needed her da.

# —3—

# A Letter Back

Kiri sprinted across the wind-rippled sand and into the sea-grape tunnels. The branches arched over the path, and the leaf-covered ground made it easier to run. She picked up speed, leaving the sounds of the gathering on the beach behind.

Snowflake perched between her shoulder blades, his whiskers brushing the nape of her neck. She'd cut the sleeves off most of her hoodies to keep them from being too warm, but when she ran through brush like this, the sharp saw-palm leaves and sea-grape twigs scratched her bare arms. Still, she didn't slow. Paulo wouldn't be able to keep Nessa and his da from fighting for long. He was counting on Kiri to bring her da back.

The air took on a foul smell from the pits where the

19

villagers buried their waste. Kiri tried holding her breath until her chest nearly burst. Then she was past the pits and into the sand oaks, cabbage palms, and sweet-smelling pines of the ghost forest.

All around her, dead trees littered the ground and scraped the sky. Most were newly dead pines, shrouded in kudzu vines. Hidden among the trees lurked a maze of concrete ruins from when this had been a city, back before the storms. The ruins made running through the ghost forest harder. Kiri jumped over the dark spaces in the rubble where pythons liked to coil, and leapt the fire ant mounds in the sandy earth. Snowflake thumped against her back, but he didn't squeak or fidget in her hood. He knew how to hunker down and hold on when she ran like this.

Gradually, the pine-needle ground softened, and mud filled the spaces between Kiri's toes. Strangler figs, banyan trees, and cypress grew here. The air became heavy and stagnant with humidity, until running felt like wading through soup—a peaty, dark soup that smelled of rotten grass and the too-sweet blooms of orchid trees.

The ghost forest was hard enough to run through, but the swamp was downright treacherous. Some patches of ground that looked solid were really soft mud pits covered by mats of algae. If she stepped on them she'd sink and drown. And there were puddles of black water where cottonmouths and gators hid. Kiri wasn't scared of the swamp, though. Every ridge, root, and rock was familiar to her, and she knew the mounds and banks to avoid, the ones where gators built their nests. She could have crossed the swamp backward with her eyes closed if she needed to.

She darted along fallen logs, jumping from one to another, then hopped onto a patchwork of saw grass that cut a zigzag path through the swamp. At last she saw her house in the distance. The plastic waller cube stood above a grassy island connected to other islands by thin spits of land and fallen logs. Because of the frequent storms and floods, the house was raised a good ten feet above the ground on stilts made to sway in the wind. Some nights, when the wind kicked up, it felt like they were on a boat. Blue spark panels glinted on the rooftop in the last rays of sunlight, and torn strips of mosquito netting billowed above the windows like Spanish moss in a breeze.

Kiri and her da were the only ones crazy enough, or "waller enough," as fugees put it, to live in the humid, mosquito-infested swamp. But none of the fugees in the stilt village had spark panels, cooling fans, or window netting like she and her da did, so none had what was needed to survive away from the wind that swept the shore and blew the mosquitoes away. And why would fugees want to live in the swamp anyway, when all the fish and salvage were offshore?

At least, that's the way everyone in the village saw it. Kiri's da thought differently about the swamp, though. Most of the things he collected for his waller customers grew here, so he'd had the wallers put their house here as well.

"Da! Da!" called Kiri as she crossed the final spit of land to the island their house stood on.

There was no response from inside. No sign of movement.

"Da!" she called again, scanning the area for the green shade hat or tan shirt her da usually wore. Martin's skin was lighter than Kiri's, and if he didn't wear long sleeves and pants during the day, he'd turn red and sore.

Kiri couldn't catch her breath to give a loud enough call. She had to stop and take several gulps of air. Then she cupped her hands around her mouth and filled her lungs.

"DAAA!"

"Kiribati?" came a faint reply.

Kiri looked around, but she didn't see Martin anywhere.

"*Kiri, Kiri-bati!*" sang her da, as if he could see her searching for him and he found it amusing.

No one, other than her da, ever called her Kiribati. Most of the fugees in the village called her Kiri or Waller Girl. She didn't mind being Kiri, but she hated being called Waller Girl. Even if her da was a waller, which was what the fugees called anyone from the walled-off city-states, she'd been born here, in the swamp. She'd never even been to a waller city.

According to her da, *Kiribati* was the name of a whole island nation that had existed once before the oceans rose and the storms increased and, like the ruins in the shallow waters off the village beach, the nation of Kiribati sank beneath the waves. Except, unlike the ruins and the other far-off ruined places where some of the fugees had come from, all of Kiribati's people, buildings, trees, animals, and every last step of land had disappeared. Most people didn't even know that such a place had ever existed. Which meant her name was like the names of the once-were creatures—a word for a lost, forgotten, perhaps imaginary thing.

Kiri raced past the house and jumped to one of the adjoining islands, following the sound of her da's singing. Every time she thought she was close, his voice seemed to come from a different direction.

*"Kiri-bati!"*

It frustrated her that her da was playing games at a time like this. "Da, I need you! The whole stilt village needs you!"

"Look up," called her da.

Kiri scanned the treetops. Three sprawling banyans stretched over the island, but most of the trees around them were cypresses. She finally spotted her da near the top of the biggest cypress. He had his tree belt on, which secured him to the trunk so he could use both hands to work.

"Come down quick!" she said.

"I'm a little busy right now," replied her da. His magnifying glasses had slid to the end of his nose and he didn't have a free hand to push them back. "This ghost orchid is extremely rare. I've been watching it grow for months, waiting for it to be ready to harvest." He held tweezers in one hand and a knife in the other as he worked to pry a silver-spotted bromeliad root from the bark of the tree.

"You have to come to the village," said Kiri. "Paulo told them you would. There's a once-were creature! It's huge!"

"Uh-huh," replied her da, clearly not listening.

"Da! It's on the beach. You need to tell the fugees what it is. Charro claimed salvage rights to it, but Nessa thinks it's a catch, and others say it's a devi!"

"A devi, huh?" said her da, still focused on the orchid roots. "Aren't those spirits?"

"Yes, but it's not a spirit. At least, I don't think it is. It's . . . it's bigger than a skiff, with black wrinkled skin and white spots like the stars at midnight. And its eyes— they're so blue, but they've gotten all sandy. You have to come right now."

"Patience, Kiribati. This is delicate work," said her da, not taking his eyes off the orchid roots. "It's already been purchased by a patron. If I let it go, the roots will break."

Kiri knew she wasn't explaining things right. If she were, he'd drop down quicker than a rotten coconut.

"I'll be there in a little bit," he added. "There's squash for dinner."

"I don't want dinner!" yelled Kiri. She looked around for some other way to get his attention. All her da thought about were the specimens his waller patrons wanted. So be it, then. She knew there was one thing he'd pay attention to.

She ran back to the stilt house, climbed the ladder to the deck, and shoved open the sliding door. The fans whirred, clearing away the day's heat, but Kiri didn't have time to enjoy the crisp coolness inside. She dug her da's spare key out of the flowerpot by the sink and raced to the sleeping loft to open the locked cabinets.

One cabinet was full of waller books sealed in plastic bags. She found a thick square book with a plain black cover and yanked it from its bag. It smelled the way rotting logs did when she rolled them over to catch millipedes.

The book was filled with pictures of hundreds of colorful fish—more fish than anyone in the village had ever seen. A few of the fragile pages tore when Kiri touched them. That's why she wasn't supposed to hold the books anymore. When she was younger her da had tried to have her read them, but the words were so long and jumbly she couldn't make much sense of them. And anyway, what was the point of knowing the names of fish that no one ever saw?

Toward the end, the book showed pictures of things other than fish—drawings of waterlords and once-were creatures. At last, Kiri found the picture she recalled seeing years ago. The creature in the drawing didn't look as big as the one on the beach, but it had a similar teardrop shape, midnight-with-stars skin, and ridged shell-like back.

Snowflake jumped from her shoulder to her bed. He sniffed the pages of the book.

"This is it," said Kiri. "This has to be it."

She sounded out each letter of the words beneath the drawing and blended them together like her da had taught her to do. Most of the kids in the fugee village couldn't read. Once, years ago, when some plastic bottles had washed ashore, Kiri tried to sound out the words on them, but when kids from the village saw her mouthing the letters they called her Waller Girl and kicked her. After that, she didn't practice reading much. Her da tried to make her do it, but when she set her mind on something, nothing could change it.

Now, though, she wished she *had* practiced, if only in secret. It took an agonizingly long time to blend the sounds into words. And even then it didn't sound right.

Snowflake nibbled on a page that had fallen out of the book. After a few test bites, he bounded across the blankets, carrying the page back to his nest.

Kiri didn't bother taking the page from him. She had more pressing things to worry about. With the book tucked under her arm, she hurried down the ladder and back to the tree her da was working in.

"It's a *letter back*!" she announced.

"A letter back?" replied her da. "Who did you send a letter to?"

Kiri opened the book and held it up for him to see. "The creature on the beach," she said. "It's a *letter back*. A *letter back turt*! You have to come down. You have to tell them what it is."

"Is that my guidebook?" Her da nearly dropped the orchid he'd been collecting. With one last tug, he separated the silver roots from the bark. Then he set the plant in a bucket attached to his harness, unstrapped the tree belt, and descended. "Kiri, you can't bring that out here! You're not even supposed to touch it. If those pages get wet—"

"It's in here, Da," she said, jabbing the drawing with her finger. She didn't care if he yelled at her or took her dinner away. At least now she had his attention. "I found it. It's a *letter back turt*!"

Her da dropped to the ground. His eyes looked stormy and his brow was knotted. He swept the book from her hands, being careful not to tear the pages like she'd done. "'Leatherback turtle,'" he read, eyes widening. "This is on the beach?"

"It's huge," said Kiri. "Charro stood on it. And it's alive!"

"That's not possible. I thought you were talking about a spirit. Are you sure this is it?"

"It looks like that, only bigger," said Kiri.

Her da started toward their house, but he was still tied to the tree. He unbuckled the harness and tossed the book, bucket, and other tools onto the grass. The ghost orchid he'd been collecting bounced out of the bucket but he didn't pause. "Show me where."

"This way!" called Kiri, edging ahead of him. "I know a quick cut."

Kiri raced along the spit of land that led to their house, eager to get back to the beach before it was too late. Already the sun had fallen beneath the horizon and the orange glow of the sky had dimmed to purple.

"Wait!" Her da suddenly turned and climbed the ladder to their house. Kiri watched him go, confused. When he came back down, he had the waller satphone and stun stick attached to his belt. Seeing them made Kiri's stomach twist. Her da never wore the stun stick, so why was he taking it now?

"Go!" he said, cutting through her daze. "Fast as you can!"

Kiri took off across the swamp, jumping from log to rubble pile to root. She looked back a few times to make sure her da was with her. His pants dripped mud and his hat had fallen off, but he didn't lag at all.

After a while, Kiri stopped glancing back and focused on crossing the swamp. The muscles in her legs ached and her lungs burned, but she didn't slow down. She wanted her da to see how fast she could run, leaping from root to log while dodging the clumps of cattails that grew in the deeper, snake-infested waters. They kept on for half an hour or so in silence.

"Good work, Kiribati," said her da when they finally reached the firmer ground of the ghost forest.

Her chest swelled with pride, not just from her father's praise but because he was with her. He'd talk to the villagers and tell them what the creature was. He'd stop them from fighting and make things okay.

The wind from the shore carried the acrid smell of smoke, along with something else—a rich, savory scent that made Kiri's mouth water. She heard music as they approached the beach. Drums, and voices singing.

At last, they made it to a path that led through the sea-grape tunnels to the dunes. Martin raced ahead. Kiri chased after him until she saw the orange glow of torches and fires in the distance.

The argument between Charro and Nessa had been settled.

# —4—

# The End of the Argument

"Paulo!" called Kiri. She spotted the skinny silhouette of her friend standing next to Tae moments after she made it to the beach. They must have been waiting near the sea-grape tunnels for her. She looked for her da, but she couldn't see him in the growing dark.

"Nessa was right!" said Paulo. "Elder Tomas ruled it a catch!"

"She wasn't right," countered Tae. "It's salvage. That's what Elder Tomas said."

"It's *both*," said Paulo. "Elder Tomas called it both, since our da couldn't drag it to shore on his own. And he couldn't take the whole thing to the boat people anyway."

"He could have. He just wanted to be generous."

Kiri edged past the brothers, unable to make sense of their excited chatter. "Where's my da?"

"Over there, by the fires." Paulo nodded to the crowd on the beach.

Almost everyone from the village was gathered there, and the mood seemed celebratory. Several people were dancing and singing, but a dark feeling stirred within Kiri when she saw fires burning near where the enormous leatherback had been.

She hurried toward the gathering, catching a glimpse of her father through the crowd. His face, lit by the orange glow of the torches, looked pale and drawn. Charro stood before him, fists clenched. Something was wrong. Kiri pushed through the crowd, fearing what might happen next.

"What have you done?" she heard her father say.

The singing stopped.

*"Da!"* called Kiri, finally making it through the crowd to the center of the gathering. But her da didn't look at her. His gaze stayed fixed on the ground near the fires.

*"What. Have. You. Done?"* he repeated. Although he sounded angry, his eyes appeared red and sad, as if he might cry.

Kiri followed his gaze. Suddenly, she understood what had made him so upset.

The enormous once-were creature lay in the sand near the fires. It wasn't moving anymore. The sand around the creature looked dark and wet. Already, parts of it were gone, and the rest was being cut up. That's why there were pots on the fires. Senek and Nessa were making soup with some of the meat, while larger slabs had been arranged around a cook fire. Charro stood shirtless nearby. His arms glistened in the firelight, wet from the work of butchering the meat.

Kiri saw other things in the sand around the dead sea turtle—bones and small white orbs that the Witch Woman collected in a bucket.

"What have you done?" said Martin, speaking the words a third time. Only this time his voice was quieter—more of a question than an accusation.

"I fed the village. That's what I've done," said Charro. "That's more than you've ever done. Now get out of my way."

Martin lifted his head to glare at the netter. "You had no right to do this."

"Who are you to speak of rights, Waller Man? You think this was yours? You think *you* had a right to this?" Charro scowled. "Typical waller. You think everything belongs to you."

"No. Not to me—"

"Then to your rich waller friends," finished Charro. "You're just angry that you didn't get to sell this to them."

Martin shook his head and blinked back tears. "You have no idea what it was worth."

"I'll learn its worth soon enough when I take the head, shell, and bones to the boat people," said Charro. He strode past Martin and filled a tin bowl with soup from one of the cook pots. "Here." He held the bowl out to Martin. "I'm *giving* this to you, because it's mine to give. And because fugees share what's needed. Now eat and let us be."

Nessa filled a second bowl and offered it to Kiri.

Kiri looked at the thick brown soup. She didn't like that the sea turtle had been killed any more than her da did. The thought of its deep blue gaze made her chest clench. She wished it could have been released, even if it was old and would have died eventually. To see such a thing and to know it might still be out there somewhere would be enough for her.

But she knew that wasn't enough for the village. People were hungry, and they couldn't pass up such a catch. That was the way of things. Fugees ate what the ocean gave them, and what they couldn't eat they sold to the boat people. That's how they survived, and there was no point making a fuss about it.

Kiri took the bowl. "Thank you," she said to Nessa.

Her da continued to stare at the remains of the sea turtle, ignoring the bowl Charro held out to him.

"Eat," said Charro.

Martin knocked the bowl aside. It tumbled to the sand, spilling soup and meat.

The crowd gasped. Even Charro looked stunned. "Are you refusing hospitality, Waller Man?"

The angry storm that had built up earlier seemed to shift to her da now. Kiri felt as if strangler fig vines were tightening around her. She looked to her da, hoping he'd apologize, but he didn't appear to realize what it meant to refuse the soup. He just kept staring at the butchered remains of the leatherback.

"He didn't mean it," said Kiri, edging between Charro and her da. "He doesn't know."

*"He knows,"* grumbled Charro. "He knows enough to steal from us. Isn't that right, Waller Man?" Charro swept something long and white off the ground and shook it in front of Martin. "You want to steal this, don't you?"

It took Kiri a moment to recognize what Charro held. Not a stick, but a bone—a sharp, splintered bone from the sea turtle.

"Steal it like you stole Laria from us?" continued Charro.

Kiri stiffened at the mention of her mother's name. No one in the village ever talked about her ma. It was bad luck to speak of the dead.

"Go home, Kiribati," said her da. His hand moved to the stun stick clipped to his belt. "I'll catch up with you shortly."

"Da, no . . . ," said Kiri.

But her father seemed too upset to listen. He stepped closer to Charro until the air between them practically crackled with tension.

"Enough sour talk," interrupted Elder Tomas. The crowd parted to let the gruff leader pass.

Relief poured through Kiri at the sight of Elder Tomas's bald head and bushy gray beard. If anyone could keep Charro and her da from fighting, it was him. He limped toward the two men, jabbing his staff into the ground with each step. A golden python decorated the end of the polished wood. In meetings, Elder Tomas raised the staff to signal for silence, and it had become as much a symbol of leadership as his shiny head.

"This is a feast," announced Elder Tomas. "We're here to celebrate our good fortune and friendship. Right, Charro? Waller Man dropped his bowl. When a guest drops a bowl, we offer him another." Elder Tomas's gaze lingered on the spot of darkened sand where the bowl Martin had knocked out of Charro's hand lay.

For a moment, no one moved. Then Paulo stepped forward, picked up the bowl, and held it out to Nessa to fill again.

Elder Tomas nodded. "Such is our way. Eat and be welcome." He eased into a chair a fugee placed for him.

Paulo had a ridiculous, missing-tooth grin on his face as he offered the bowl of soup to Martin. Kiri couldn't keep herself from smiling back at her friend. Maybe things would be okay after all.

But her da still didn't take the bowl.

The strangler-fig vines cinched tighter, choking Kiri. Why was her da doing this? Why couldn't he just eat the soup like everyone else? Why did he always have to be different?

"Take it," she said, nudging her da. If he ate the soup he'd be a guest, and guests were protected. Charro wouldn't be able to fight him then. "Please. Eat the soup."

Martin looked at her with a perplexed, distant expression. "We won't be part of this, Kiribati."

He grabbed her hand and tugged her toward the ghost forest. Soup slopped out of her bowl.

Charro sneered. "See? He doesn't respect us. He just wants to take what's ours and tell us what to do. He takes and takes and doesn't give back, like he took Laria. . . ."

Martin turned and glared at Charro.

"Like he took her and killed her," said Charro.

Something in Kiri's da snapped. He stepped toward Charro, and Charro shoved him. Soon the two men were grappling near the fire, each struggling for advantage. Their faces wrinkled and orange light reflected off their eyes.

The storm had finally broken, and a hungry bloodlust took hold of the villagers. Fugees shouted, while Elder Tomas sat mute, permitting the fight to continue—all because her da had refused the soup.

"Stop!" yelled Kiri. She lunged between Charro and her da to break up the fight.

An elbow jostled her shoulder and a hand tried to push her out of the way. Then something scratched her cheek. It all happened too quickly, like being tumbled by a rogue wave. Kiri fell back on the sand. Her face stung and her vision blurred. She blinked several times, rubbing her eyes, and her fingers came away sticky with blood. It took her a moment to figure out why. The bone Charro held, with its sharp, splintered end, must have cut her.

Charro looked down at her in bewilderment.

"Kiribati?" said her da. He knelt next to her.

"I'm fine." She swallowed, doing her best not to cry in front of everyone. "It's just a scratch."

Her da brushed her wild hair back from her face. "You're bleeding."

"That child is always in the way," grumbled Charro.

Martin whirled to his feet. "Get away from her!"

"Or what?" challenged Charro. "This is your fault, Waller Man."

Martin slid the stun stick from the holster on his belt. It made a high, angry buzz as it powered up.

*"Enough!"* shouted Elder Tomas.

The enraged leader's gaze swept the crowd. "You!" He pointed the end of his staff at Kiri and her da. "Leave. You wallers aren't welcome here anymore."

Kiri was too shocked to move. This wasn't supposed to happen. She'd brought her da to the village to help. He was supposed to stop a fight, not start one.

Her da lifted her to her feet, but she squirmed out of his hands. She refused to let him carry her.

"Come on, Kiribati," he said.

He took her hand and guided her back toward the seagrape tunnels. Kiri stumbled a few times. The air felt too thick to breathe and the sting of her scratched cheek made her eyes water. Her da kept his arm under hers to catch her if she fell.

"We'll go home and take care of that cut," he said. "You'll be okay. You did good, coming to get me. If only

I'd gotten here sooner." He shook his head and sighed. "It was a female," he added, as if explaining could somehow make things better. "They're supposed to be extinct. It's probably been at sea for decades looking for a mate. They only come to shore to nest. You understand? It might have been the last, and after all these years it was coming here *to nest. . . ."*

They'd nearly reached the sea-grape tunnels when Kiri looked back. No one, other than her da, was talking. The crowd gathered by the fires had become crushingly silent. No music, drumming, or singing. It was the suffocating silence of two hundred people who hated them now.

Kiri wanted to tell them she wasn't a waller. Not like her da. She was a fugee like them. How could things have gone so wrong?

Paulo's skinny form stood by the edge of the group, silhouetted by the distant firelight. He gave her a feeble wave—the sort of wave people gave to netters who headed off when the sky turned gray and no one else was foolish enough to paddle out.

Kiri couldn't bring herself to wave back.

# —5—

# Scars

"You'll probably have a scar," said her da as he cleaned the cut on Kiri's cheek. "Good thing Charro missed your eye."

Each dab of peroxide hurt worse than a dozen fire-ant stings, but Kiri didn't cry. She wanted her da to see that she wasn't a child anymore. She was old enough to make her own decisions, and she wouldn't mess things up like he did.

Of course, he didn't see this. Just like he didn't see why he should have eaten the soup, or the looks of contempt on the fugees' faces when they'd walked away. There were so many things, she now realized, that he didn't see.

"Sea turtles always return to the beach where they were born to nest," her da said, still talking about his work. "They can be gone for decades. Then, one day, they'll come back to lay their eggs in the sand. But now it's gone. Maybe all of them are." He clenched his jaw, looking pained, until he seemed to remember that Kiri was the one who'd been hurt. "Perhaps," he continued, "if I collect the right specimens, I'll be able to take you to a clinic in the city. They have stims that can erase a scar, and then it'll be like this whole thing never happened. How's that sound?"

Kiri glared at him. She didn't care about the stupid scar. What did a scar matter if she couldn't go to the village anymore? Besides, it wasn't like he'd be able to take her to a fancy waller clinic anyway. The wallers wouldn't let her through the city gates—not without a waller mark on her arm like he had. And the only way to get a waller mark was to be born in the city in the first place, which she had not been.

"Get some sleep," he said, dabbing the cut on her cheek one last time. "Tomorrow things will . . ." His voice trailed off. They both knew things wouldn't be better. The once-were creature was dead, and most of the villagers were angry at them.

"You'll heal," he finally said. He kissed her forehead and sent her up the ladder to the sleeping loft.

※

For a long time, Kiri lay awake, watching the blades of the cooling fan spin while the whir of gears in the hand generator filtered up from the room below. After a few minutes, her da stopped cranking the generator and turned on the music player. Kiri heard the muted notes of the strange, voiceless waller music he preferred. It sounded like thousands of different-sized stones falling on metal ruins. The tiny, unnatural notes chased each other up and down in cascading patterns. He'd told her once that it was old music, from a time before the storms and walled-off cities, which made Kiri wonder what people had been like back then, and why they'd make music that you couldn't sing or dance to.

Snowflake hopped across the blanket. His whiskers tickled as he sniffed her wound. When he started licking it with his tiny, rough tongue, she jerked her head away, frightening him.

"Sorry, Snowflake," whispered Kiri. She knew he was only trying to help.

The little rat groomed his fur instead. *If you don't want me to clean you, I'll clean myself,* he seemed to say. He worked from his ears down to the tip of his nose, but there was a spot at the back of his neck that he couldn't reach.

Kiri stroked him behind his ears, and Snowflake finally appeared to relax. He stretched out, making soft snuffling sounds.

Most of Snowflake's fur was the brown color of dry cabbage-palm leaves, where wild rats liked to nest. Kiri had found him beneath one such tree when he was a pup. At first she thought he'd fallen out of the nest, but he had bites and scratches from other rats, so maybe he'd been kicked out. That was why she'd taken him home and cared for him. He was an outsider, like her.

She named him Snowflake because of the odd star-shaped patch of white fur between his eyes. Kiri's da had told her stories about snow, claiming that when he was a kid, he played in piles of it. She couldn't imagine frozen water ever falling from the sky in delicate six-pointed stars, but she liked the stories, and she liked the sound of the word *snowflake*. It seemed a suitably improbable name for an improbable creature, which was another thing they had in common.

The music player crackled and faded to silence as the generator-cells ran out. Not long after, the ladder creaked beneath her father's weight.

Kiri closed her eyes and lay still. Snowflake curled in the space between her shoulder and neck. The room brightened for a moment when her da pulled back the loft curtain. Kiri pretended to be asleep while he climbed over to his side of the loft.

When at last she heard his deep, hushed snores coming from the other side of the loft, she pushed back her covers and crept toward the ladder. Snowflake bounded after her and cocked his head. She could almost hear him say, *Did you think I'd let you go without me?*

Kiri grabbed her sleeveless hoodie and held it open until the rat clambered in. Improbable outsiders like them needed to stick together.

The hardest part of sneaking out was crossing the kitchen floor. She grabbed her tire sandals, but didn't put them on. Bare feet were quieter. Stepping carefully, she avoided all the boards that creaked. The only sound was the hum of the cooling fans and her father's deep breaths. So far, so good.

She slid open the outer door and tiptoed onto the deck. Her da always raised the chain ladder at night. She tried not to let the metal links clank against the deck as she lowered the ladder and climbed down. Once she reached the ground, she strapped on her sandals and set off for the village.

The cut on her cheek began to sting and bleed again when she ran, but she didn't slow her pace. She hoped the cut *would* leave a scar. A long, thick pink scar. All the netters had scars—rope burns up and down their arms from hauling in nets, and slashes from hooks and jellyfish stings. Her ma had probably had scars like that, too. Scars told you who you were and where you came from.

Elder Tomas was wrong to call her a waller. She'd show him and all the others that she was a fugee, same as her ma.

*Steal it like you stole Laria from us,* thought Kiri, remembering what Charro had said. It was one of the only times she'd ever heard a fugee say her mother's name.

Kiri had just a few wave-worn memories of her mother. She knew her ma's parents had died in a scav raid. And she knew her ma had lived in the village and gone out on the skiffs to pull in the nets and crab traps.

According to her da, her ma was the only netter who helped him when he came to the village to collect specimens. He said she talked to the other netters for him because most fugees thought he spoke funny and were afraid to answer his questions. But not Laria. She was daring and wild, and, as Kiri's da put it, nothing could hold her back.

Not long after he arrived, Laria moved to the swamp to live with him.

*He took her and killed her,* thought Kiri, recalling the other thing Charro had said.

The red fever killed her mother—that's what her da had told her. But what if there was more to the story?

The thought made Kiri uneasy. She stumbled, nearly slipping off a log into a patch of black water where cotton-mouths liked to nest.

Kiri tried to push Charro's words from her mind. The red fever had killed her ma—that's all. Since her da was a waller, he didn't have to worry about catching the fever. Wallers were protected from illnesses like that. But her ma wasn't, and wallers never let fugees into their cities.

Maybe that's why fugees hated wallers. While fugees got sick, starved, and watched storms and scavs destroy their homes, wallers stayed safe behind their city walls and did nothing. They let countless fugees die.

Kiri reached firmer ground. She kicked the mud off her sandals and began to run again. In the moonlight, she spotted the back of what looked like a sleeping gator on a grassy ridge ahead. She probably should have taken another route, but this was the fastest way. Kiri raced toward the dark form. It was definitely a gator, and a big one at that.

She leapt over it, landed on the other side, and kept running. With any luck, the feast wouldn't be over. Fugee celebrations sometimes went until sunrise. When she got there, she'd ask for a bowl of soup and eat it in front of everyone to prove that she wasn't a waller. Then everyone would see she really was her mother's daughter, and Nessa might take her in. And in the morning she could go out on a skiff and pull in the nets like her mother had done. She could earn a catch share, and finally have a place in the village, and never be called Waller Girl again.

It was thoughts like this that spurred Kiri on, despite how tired she felt. By the time she made it to the ghost forest, the moon had moved a few fingers across the sky. Fortunately, enough light reflected off the clouds to keep her from tripping over rubble.

At last she smelled it—smoke seeping inland from the fires on the beach, and the salty, dark scent of the soup. She slowed and listened. In the distance, she could barely hear the breaking of waves and the faint rise and fall of laughter, but the forest around her had suddenly become too quiet. Even the crickets stopped chirping. Snowflake curled into a tight ball, deep in her hood, as if he sensed it too. They weren't alone anymore.

Kiri paused and glanced back. She thought she saw a shadow move at the edge of her vision. As soon as she looked, it stopped. She scanned the forest, studying the shadows carefully.

There, near a palmetto, one of the shadows moved again. Or was it just the wind blowing a branch? It had to be the wind.

"Who's there?" she asked.

No answer.

"I know you're there. You don't scare me."

Still nothing. She continued on, annoyed that she'd let

fear get the better of her. Fugees weren't afraid of the dark. Only wallers clung to lights and thought darkness was bad.

But as she stepped, the shadow stepped with her.

"I see you," she said.

The shadow paused again. If it was just the wind, then why did it stop when she spoke?

Kiri's pulse skipped. She took a few more steps and the shadow approached, fluid and ghost silent. Soon it would reach her.

"Hold tight, Snowflake," she whispered.

The little rat burrowed deeper into her hood.

She bolted toward the sea-grape tunnels. They weren't very far off. If she could make it through the sea grapes, she'd reach the dunes and the open beach, where other people were. She'd be safe then and could laugh at whatever had spooked her. She just had to make it to the beach.

Something slammed into her shoulder. Time stuttered and slowed as claws pierced her flesh and pulled her down.

Kiri started to scream, but when she hit the ground, stumbling and rolling, her breath whooshed out and the scream died in her throat.

A shadow hovered over her, its broad head blocking out the night sky. Hot breath scalded her skin as the shadow sniffed at her neck. Kiri felt jolted from her body. She lay perfectly still, staring at the shadow creature's wide, yellow-green eyes—eyes that gleamed in the moonlight with wild intelligence.

Whispers filled her head. Although Kiri couldn't understand exactly what the whispers said, she felt them calling to her, urging her to listen. She remembered an elder in the village saying once that a powerful connection flowed between predator and prey at the moment of death. Hunters needed to respect what they hunted, and they needed to connect to it to kill it. Perhaps that's what this was— the whispery connection that would bring her end. But in the shadow creature's gaze, Kiri saw something other than death. Something closer to kinship.

Firelight pushed back the dark, followed by a woman's sharp cry. "Sheee!" shouted the woman. "Sheee! Sheee!"

The shadow glanced to the side and Kiri saw that its tawny head was twice as wide as hers, with spear-tip ears and a stout muzzle. It bared long, pointed teeth.

The woman shouted again, waving her torch. Quick as liquid through open fingers, the creature vanished into the forest.

Several seconds passed before Kiri realized she wasn't breathing. She opened her mouth, forcing her lungs to fill with air again. It felt as if her life had already left her and she was only now tugging it back.

Her breath returned in ragged fits, like a net caught on rocks. She wheezed and coughed. Pain from her shoulder surged through her as she tried to sit up. It hurt so much that her vision blurred and she fell back again.

"Waller Girl?" said the Witch Woman, leaning over her with the torch. "Great gods, child. What are you doing here?"

# —6—

# Words Long Forgotten

*Hush, my child, don't you fear*
*When thunder rumbles, the rain is near.*

Kiri heard a woman's voice singing. It sounded far away at first, and as raspy as dry palm leaves rustling in a breeze. She tried to open her eyes, but her body felt distant and detached. It took a few seconds before she could get her eyelids to move, and when they finally fluttered open, sunlight spilled in, blinding her. Her head reeled and she had to shut her eyes again.

*Don't try to fly like a broken-winged dove*
*They all fall down and drown in the mud.*

The voice sounded closer now. Softer. This time Kiri opened her eyes only a sliver, to let them adjust to the brightness. Colors swirled around her, gradually coalescing into the figure of a woman with several thin black braids cascading around her face.

*Hear the crickets chirping in the grass*
*When the wind blows the clouds come fast.*

The woman leaned over and pressed a wet cloth to Kiri's forehead and cheeks. It felt blissfully cool against her skin.

*Little crickets know how to hop*
*While the rains go drip-drip drop.*

Even better than the cool cloth, though, was the sense of being cared for. As the woman sang and dabbed the cloth against her forehead, Kiri's chest swelled with warmth. Her da never sang to her—not like this. And he wouldn't have pressed a cool cloth to her head either. What she felt was something else entirely. Something she'd had a name for once, but hadn't spoken aloud in years.

The name rose from the dark depths of memory and swept across her tongue. "Ma?"

"Shhh . . . I'm here, Cricket," replied her mother.

She looked just like she did in the vids her da had shown Kiri. Her eyes were dark and kind. Her lips curled up in a wry smile, and a few of the black braids sprouting from a cluster on her head fell across her cheeks. The resemblance was so striking that Kiri thought she must have been watching a vid, except her ma hadn't called her Cricket in any of the vids. But as soon as her ma said it now, voice lilting over the syllables in a musical way, like the sound of a door unlocking—*Crick-et*—Kiri remembered her mother calling her this hundreds of times before. A true memory.

"I thought you were dead." Kiri kept her eyes half-open, not daring to move and disrupt whatever vision she was having.

Her mother dabbed the wet cloth against the cut on her cheek, wiping off the blood. It stung a little, but it also felt real, and for that reason, wonderful.

Kiri tried to sit up, no longer afraid to move. She needed to hold her mother and keep her here.

"Easy, Cricket," said her ma, placing her palm against Kiri's forehead. "You should sleep now."

Kiri lay back, confused. "Am *I* dead?" she asked. That was the only explanation for how this could be happening. She must be in the land of the dead, where her mother had been waiting for her.

"No. You've been marked."

Kiri frowned. "Marked? Why?"

"That's not for me to say." Her mother picked up a small glass bottle and poured a few drops into a cup. "But *you* know. Or you will. You wouldn't have been chosen otherwise. That's why I gave you the knife."

"What knife?"

"The knife I've been keeping for you. I stitched its sheath to your belt."

Kiri reached down and felt a sheath of smoothly worn leather attached to her belt, and the stiff handle of a knife against her hip. Touching the knife comforted her and made her feel older. All the netters carried knives like this for cutting lines and gutting fish.

"One who's brave enough to be marked by the Shadow That Hunts is brave enough to carry a blade," said her ma. "Just remember, a knife isn't only for cutting. In skilled hands, it can also mend. Now drink." She held the cup to Kiri's lips.

Kiri was so thirsty, she took a sip without asking what it was. The bitter liquid made her mouth pucker and her throat burn.

"It stings," she said.

"That's why you need to drink, Cricket."

Kiri swallowed a few more burning sips. The liquid trailed fire down her throat, warming her stomach.

Her mother nodded, pleased. Then she put the cap on the bottle and stood.

"Don't go! Ma!" cried Kiri.

Her mother looked back, only now she appeared thin and wrinkled. Her hands were gnarled as driftwood. "Poor child," she said. "You're too young to speak to the dead."

In place of her mother stood an old woman with cloudy eyes and gray, stringy hair.

"Where is she?" asked Kiri. "What did you do with her?"

Kiri thought she must have been looking at the wrong person, but when she tried to search the room for her mother, a wave of dizziness overtook her. The warmth from whatever she'd drunk spread through her body, pulling her down.

"She was here," muttered Kiri. "She was right here. Bring her back."

The Witch Woman shook her head and gave her a sad look. "Rest, child," she said. "You've been marked for a reason, and you're going to need your strength."

The next time Kiri woke, it was to the sound of people arguing.

"She's twice marked," said the Witch Woman. "You know what that means?"

Kiri struggled to open her eyes. It was so bright she had to force herself to squint and focus on something until the dizziness passed. Finally, her pupils adjusted and she saw Snowflake's brown back. The rat was curled on her hoodie, near her head. Even asleep he wouldn't leave her side. Beyond him, she noticed the ankles and feet of several people standing on the sand. Other people were sitting on overturned buckets next to piles of nets. The air smelled of seaweed and rotten jellies, and the sunlight glowed blue from the tarp tied to poles overhead.

She was in the mending tent, where netters came during the heat of the day to untangle their lines and mend their nets. Nessa was there, along with Senek, the Witch Woman, and a few other fugees she couldn't see. She had no idea how she'd gotten here, or why she lay on a straw mat in the mending tent instead of in her own bed.

"You and your portents, woman," said a gruff voice. It must have been Charro speaking. Kiri spotted his hairy calves and dirty feet on one side of the mending tent. "A feral cat scratched her, that's all. The girl has a way of finding trouble."

"No. The Shadow That Hunts marked her. I saw it with my own eyes."

"You had too much palm wine."

"We all had too much palm wine," mumbled someone else.

"There is no *Shadow That Hunts*," continued Charro. "It was just an overgrown feral heading for the waste pits."

Kiri tried to turn her head to see more. Her cheek stung, sending another wave of dizziness through her, and her eyes were unable to catch up with her movements.

"I'm telling you, it was no feral," asserted the Witch Woman. "She's been marked. Once by a devi of the water, and once by a devi of the land."

Charro snickered. "Hear that, Senek? Crazy old woman thinks I'm a devi."

"Not you," said the Witch Woman. "The bone of the creature you killed. *That's* what marked her. That's the devi I speak of."

"If that was a devi, then I'll be a rich man when the

tide turns and I trade its head, shell, and bones to the boat people," said Charro.

"I warned you not to kill it," continued the Witch Woman. "I warned you to let it go. Now there's been a second portent."

"Why two portents?" asked Nessa. "I thought portents came in threes."

"They do," said the Witch Woman. "So we best pay attention now, or a sky devi will mark her as well. And if we don't listen then, death will follow."

"Death might come, but not for us," said Charro. "It'll come for her. That's all that mark on her back means. A feral cat attacked her, and if the wounds are bad they'll get infected and make her sick. The sort of sickness you don't wake from."

"Quiet!" said Nessa. "She'll hear you."

"I'm only saying the truth," grumbled Charro. "I've seen it happen before. So have you."

Nessa said something to Charro that Kiri didn't hear. Then Tae's voice cut through the group. "Waller Man's coming," he said. "Paulo and I saw him in the ghost forest."

Kiri sucked in a breath, realizing they were talking about her da. She attempted to move her arms and push herself off the ground, but her muscles barely responded. She felt as weak as a jellyfish on sand.

"Shhh, child," said the Witch Woman, kneeling next to her. "Save your strength."

Kiri opened her eyes fully. Several fugees were staring down at her like she was something foul that had washed ashore.

The tarp rustled as someone else entered.

"What happened?" asked her da. "What did you do to her?" He took the Witch Woman's place by Kiri's side.

"Only what I'd do for one of my own," replied the Witch Woman.

Kiri tried to sit up, but the effort made everything spin. At least she could feel her body now. One hand tingled with pins and needles, and her right shoulder itched terribly.

"It might take some time for the sleeping oils to leave her system," said the Witch Woman.

"Sleeping oils?" asked her da, sounding distraught.

"She was squirming too much. I had to clean out her wounds."

Martin turned to confront the Witch Woman. "I've told you, you have no idea what's in those concoctions you use. . . ."

Kiri finally managed to sit all the way up. The blanket slid down and the breeze felt good against her sweaty skin, but the itch at her shoulder grew worse.

She reached to scratch it and felt a square cloth stuck to her, right where the itch was. With a sharp tug, she yanked the cloth free. Blood stained the fabric. The Witch Woman must have fixed the cloth to her shoulder as a bandage.

She heard a gasp behind her and turned. Paulo stood at

the edge of the mending tent, staring at her wide-eyed and slack-jawed.

"I was coming back to eat the soup," she said, thinking Paulo must be surprised to see her after she'd been kicked out the other night. That would explain his shocked expression. "I would have eaten it . . . ," she added.

Paulo shook his head. "Da! Tae! Look . . ." He pointed to Kiri's bare shoulder.

Several of the adults stopped arguing. Their mouths fell open like Paulo's had as they stared at the wound on Kiri's shoulder.

"You still think it was only a feral cat that scratched her, Charro?" asked the Witch Woman. "I don't know about you, but I've never seen a cat with paws as big as my hand."

# –7–

## Tracks

Her da wanted to carry her home, but Kiri shrugged off his help. She didn't want to look childish in front of the whole village. Besides, with every step her head grew clearer and the tingling in her hands and feet lessened. Martin stayed by her side, carrying her hoodie with Snowflake in it as they shuffled across the beach toward the ghost forest.

The Witch Woman was taking everyone to see where she'd found Kiri the night before, and where she'd seen the Shadow That Hunts. Word of the enormous claw marks on Kiri's shoulder had spread through the village, and most fugees who weren't out in their skiffs followed the Witch Woman.

"This way," said the elder woman. She cut between two sand dunes toward the sea-grape tunnels. Kiri noticed a patch of disturbed sand near the base of one of the dunes, as if someone had dug a hole there and then filled it in. The Witch Woman hurried past the dunes, directing the fugees to a different area.

"I was making my way to the waste pits when I heard a scream," said the Witch Woman. "So I took my torch and ran to help. That's when I saw the Shadow That Hunts. It stood over her, eyes blazing like swamp fire in the dark."

The Witch Woman pointed to where Kiri had been pinned beneath the huge shadow creature at the edge of the ghost forest. Nessa, Charro, and a few other fugees stepped closer to investigate.

"Look!" said Nessa, pointing to tracks in the muddy ground. "The devi stood here!"

Several more fugees tramped closer to see the tracks.

A tremble coursed through Kiri as she recalled the prickle of the creature's whiskers on her neck. The Shadow That Hunts was real.

"Stay back! You'll ruin the trail," said Martin. He left Kiri's side to investigate the paw prints. "It's easily nine centimeters across," he announced, measuring one print with the blade of his knife. "Three-lobed heel pad. No toenail marks . . . This is incredible!"

Martin dug around in one of his pockets for a camera.

"Keep your waller hands off it," said Charro. "You shouldn't even be here. The devi is ours."

"This track wasn't made by a devi or a spirit or whatever other nonsense you believe," said Martin. "It was made by a panther. It probably smelled the blood from the sea turtle you slaughtered." He aimed his camera and took several short vids of the tracks.

Other fugees crowded in to get a better look. Some stepped so close that the muddy ground shifted and filled in parts of the prints. Eager villagers forced Kiri and her da aside.

Kiri wandered farther into the ghost forest, vaguely remembering where the panther had gone when it had run off. She found a couple more tracks in a patch of sandy dirt, but she didn't say anything about them. Growing still, she listened to the villagers' chatter behind her.

"A panther?" asked Nessa. "I heard about those once years ago. Didn't think any were left."

"Almost no one did," said Kiri's da. "Except me."

"How much is one of those worth?" asked Senek.

"*Worth?*" replied her da. He sounded disturbed by the question.

"What would the wallers trade for it?" pressed Nessa. "A boat?"

"You can't trade it. Not like that."

"He's lying," said Senek. "You saw him take those vids. He wants to sell it to the wallers himself."

"Forget the wallers," said Charro. "We should trap it and go to the boat people with it. They'll buy the skin, teeth, claws, and liver. They'll even buy the bones. They grind them up and make medicine out of them. I bet they'd pay enough to feed the whole village for a year."

"Is that true?" asked Nessa.

Kiri glanced back, and saw her da shake his head vehemently. "No. That's not . . ." He shuffled his feet, stepping on the tracks. Kiri realized he was intentionally destroying them so the fugees couldn't follow the trail. "You can't kill it."

"You don't get to tell us what we can or can't do, Waller Man," said Charro. "Elder Tomas made it clear you're not welcome here anymore. If I see you again, it won't end well for you."

"Relax. We're going," said her da.

Kiri considered telling the fugees about the tracks she'd found. They'd be grateful to her. They might even let her stay in the village. But she didn't speak.

Instead, she swept her foot across the sandy ground and wiped out the tracks like her da had done. Maybe the Witch Woman was right. Maybe the panther *was* a devi and it had chosen her for some purpose. What that purpose was, she couldn't say. She just knew that she didn't want anyone to trap and kill the panther like they'd killed the sea turtle.

Martin called to her and Kiri hurried after him. When they were far enough inland that the fugees couldn't hear them, he got out his satphone and typed several numbers into it.

"Have to act fast," he said. "I'll need cameras. Spider steel. Shock pods. Motion detectors . . ." He kept listing items as he sent vids of the paw print to his waller patrons.

The claw marks on Kiri's shoulder itched. She touched the wound, wincing from the pain. Knowing the panther was out there changed things. Even now, in the safety of daylight, picturing the panther in the woods made her heart swell with fear and awe, and something else. It was because of the panther that she'd seen her mother. Kiri couldn't explain how or why, but the panther had connected her to something greater.

She considered telling her da about the vision she'd had of her mother, but she decided not to. He might not believe her.

*You've been marked for a reason,* she thought, recalling the Witch Woman's words.

If that was true, then maybe it was no accident she'd seen which direction the tracks led. She might have been marked to follow the tracks and find the panther.

And if she found the panther, perhaps she'd find her mother again, too.

# —8—

# Severed

A dragonfly searching for a lily pad to land on—that's what Kiri thought the waller craft resembled as it neared the beach. It spiraled down from the sky with swift, insect-like movements. Instead of wings, it had two whirring thrust pods and a third thrust pod at the end of its metal tail.

"A tridrone," Kiri's da called it, but Kiri preferred to think of it as a giant dragonfly. The camera lenses and other sensors on the bulbous head shimmered in the sunlight like dragonfly eyes. And the sound of it reminded her of a thousand mosquitoes buzzing.

They were as far down the beach from the fugee village as they could go, near the rocky point beyond which the coast became an uncrossable labyrinth of mangrove swamps and mud channels. Even so, the fugees would see the tridrone's descent. How could they not? The whirring sound of the thrust pods carried across the breaking waves, and the sunlight glinted off its metal sides.

It was only a matter of time before fugees came to investigate. Her da kept glancing up the beach and fiddling with the stun stick strapped to his belt.

"Be ready to carry as much as you can," he said. "Once we get the drop, head back to our meeting spot in the ghost forest. Don't wait for me and don't look back. Just take the supplies and go. Okay, Kiribati?"

Kiri nodded. It had been almost two days since the panther had marked her, and most of the wound had closed. Still, it stung when she moved and it itched constantly. There was no way she could wear a strap across her hurt shoulder, so she hadn't been able to bring a backpack like her da. She hadn't been able to bring Snowflake, either. Her da said the rat would only get in the way. Not having Snowflake made Kiri uneasy. She kept reaching back to pet him, but he wasn't there.

At last, the tridrone hovered above the landing spot. It turned from side to side, searching the area.

"Stay here until it's down and the blades stop spinning," said her da. He left the shelter of the ghost forest and held his satphone up.

The metal dragonfly descended in front of him. Wind from its thrust pods blew off his hat and made his shirt flap back.

Seeing it close, Kiri was surprised that the tridrone wasn't bigger. She wondered if the wallers were small enough to cram themselves into the coffin-sized, window-less body. Then she remembered her da explaining that it was too dangerous for waller pilots to come here, so they flew their sky skiffs remotely, peering into vid screens in their far-off city.

The tridrone came to rest on four spindly legs. As soon as the red light on top turned green, the whirring sound lessened and her da stepped toward it, careful not to get too close to the spinning blades of the thrust pods.

Martin tapped a series of numbers into a pad on the dragonfly's head and a door at the front yawned open. Reaching into the tridrone's mouth, he pulled out boxes and other supplies, which he tossed onto the beach. There were many big rolls of spider steel wire. From Martin's expression, Kiri knew they must be heavy. And expensive. She'd never seen this much shining metal before. Then he pulled out a bundle of metal poles for some sort of structure, along with more cardboard boxes. Kiri couldn't believe how much stuff the tridrone had brought. The supplies spread out on the beach probably cost more than all the skiffs in the village combined.

Her da waved to her and she hurried over to carry stuff back.

"Hold on," he muttered, reaching into the dark mouth of the tridrone again. "We're missing a few things."

"What things?" asked Kiri.

Shouts from up the beach pulled Martin's attention away before he could respond. Already, six or seven fugees were running toward them. Kiri couldn't make out who they were, but she hoped Charro wasn't among them. With any luck, most of the netters would be too far offshore to return this quickly.

"This better be it," said her da, sliding a black case from the dragonfly body. He flipped two latches on the case and opened it, revealing a long black barrel and other metal parts.

Her da set to work assembling the rifle. Although Kiri had never seen one before, she knew that's what it was. She'd heard plenty of older kids talk about the guns that wallers, scavs, and boat people carried. Some kids even carved fake guns out of sticks and made a game of pretending to shoot each other. But no one in the village had a waller rifle like this, with a long barrel and a fancy far-sight tube on top.

Fugees weren't allowed to have guns. Only wallers were permitted to carry them, and if you walked too close to their city walls, they'd shoot you full of holes. Scav raiders and boat people had guns, too, but theirs were shorter and uglier. Scav guns could be plenty deadly, though. Fugees always retreated to the ghost forest whenever they spotted an unfamiliar boat offshore. Without weapons of their own, they didn't have a chance of fending off raiders.

"What are you going to do?" asked Kiri as her da snapped the barrel into place and fixed it with a knob.

"Only what I have to," he said.

"You're not going to hurt them, are you?"

"It's just a tranquilizer gun, but don't tell them that." He pulled back a latch on the side of the gun and peered into the chamber. The fugees were little more than a stone's throw away and coming fast. Then he searched the case for something else, grabbing a black plastic rectangle with several metal darts in it.

Martin cursed and snapped the darts into the bottom of the rifle, right as the dragonfly tridrone started to beep loudly. A moment later, the thrust pods hummed and the blades began to spin.

"Get back! Now!" said her da.

A crackle of pain shot across Kiri's shoulder as she grabbed what boxes she could and scooted back. The blades of the thrust pods whirred, kicking up clouds of stinging sand. Instead of backing away from the tridrone, her da seemed to be fighting to hold down the mouth door.

"There must be another box!" He frantically searched the cargo hold.

The metal dragonfly tail lifted off the ground and the tridrone tipped dangerously toward Martin. Still, he didn't let go. "You can't do this!" he yelled. "Not again!"

The whir of the thrust pods increased, becoming an angry scream. Clouds of sand engulfed Martin as the fugees neared.

Senek, red-faced and panting, carried an old fishing net. He swung the weighted ends of the net over his head, preparing to throw it.

"Da! Look out!" shouted Kiri.

Her da glanced at Senek and his hand slipped off the front of the tridrone. Instantly, the metal dragonfly shot into the air, becoming little more than a dot high above them in a few heartbeats. Kiri watched it go, amazed by its speed, until a shout from one the fugees called her attention back to earth.

"Waller!" yelled Senek, still swinging his net. He shuffled toward Martin, along with a few other fugees—mostly kids and women who hadn't gone out on the skiffs that morning. "You were warned not to come back here. That's ours by rights." He nodded to the boxes on the beach. "Everything on this beach is ours."

Her da cocked the rifle. Most of the fugees stopped then, but sunburned, red-faced Senek kept stepping closer, swinging his net.

*CRACK!*

The shot sprayed up sand in front of Senek. He jumped back and the weighted ends of the net slapped his shoulders.

"We're going to gather our things and go," said Kiri's da. He cocked the rifle again and aimed at Senek. "Don't make me use this. Next time I won't miss."

Senek's expression seemed to melt until his eyes became two thin slits in his sweating face. "The others are gonna hear about this."

"Kiribati," said her da, "take what boxes you can and head to our meeting spot."

Kiri did as she was told. Even though her da sounded calm, there was an edge to his words that frightened her.

She looked back once she reached the ghost forest. Her da had managed to load most of the remaining supplies into his backpack. Then he slung the pack over his shoulder and lifted the last box with his other arm, all while keeping the waller rifle pointed at Senek.

Kiri and her da stashed the supplies they carried in the ghost forest. Then Martin unwound a strand of spider steel and attached it to a black box that he nailed to the trunk of a tree.

"Take this," he said, handing Kiri the heavy spool of spider steel. "Walk north with it. We need to put up a fence before the netters return and find out what we've done."

*You mean what* you've *done,* thought Kiri.

"Hurry!" urged her da.

Kiri headed north through the trees and scattered ruins of the ghost forest, letting the wire unspool behind her with every step. The spider steel was so thin she could barely see it, but it was stronger than the heaviest fishing line.

Her da wore gloves as he worked, securing spider steel around tree branches and palm trunks, forming a messy web that went from the forest floor to as far up as he could reach. Every now and then he nailed an orange warning sign to a tree on the beach side of the wires. Sweat poured down his sides as he worked, but he didn't slow.

"Faster!" he said to Kiri, checking the position of the sun. "I need more wire."

After a while, Kiri finished uncoiling the second spool of spider steel. Her da attached the end to a black box that he nailed to the back of a tree about six feet up. Then he pulled another spool from his backpack, undid the end, and gave it to Kiri to walk with. His hands shook and blood from several cuts trickled down his arms. The cuts were from brushing against strands of spider steel. Kiri hated to imagine what would happen if someone didn't see the wire and ran into it.

She peered back at what she and her da had done so far. Silver wires glinted in the fading sunlight, forming a nearly invisible razor web between the ghost forest and the beach. They'd strung up half a mile or so of wire, and they were almost to the main path she used when she ran through the ghost forest and sea-grape tunnels to collect seawater samples every day. Once the fence was up, she wouldn't be able to cross anymore. Realizing this made Kiri feel hot and trapped, like a fish stuck in a shrinking tide pool.

She stumbled, delirious. The scratches on her shoulder and cheek burned and her legs felt weak.

Her da gave her a concerned look. "You okay?" He handed her his water bottle. "Drink something."

Kiri tilted the bottle and drank, but the hot, light-headed feeling didn't go away.

Her da got out another black box from his pack and began to attach it to the next spool of wire. "I'm sorry about all this, Kiribati. You'll be able to rest in a bit, but right now we have to get this fence up."

"I don't want a fence," said Kiri. "How am I supposed to get to the beach if there's a fence in the way?"

"You won't," said her da. "Not anymore. It's not safe for you to go to the beach anymore."

Kiri stiffened, struck by her father's reply. "Not ever? Are you saying I can't ever go back to the beach?"

Her da brushed his hair from his face with a gloved hand. "I don't know, Kiribati. Maybe, once I catch the panther, I'll be able to patch things up with the villagers and then we can take down the fence. But right now this is the only way to save the panther."

"Save it?" Kiri frowned. "How's a fence going to save it? You're just like Charro and the others. You just want to trap it and trade it for whatever you can get."

"No, Kiribati, that's not it at all. *I'm* putting up this fence to protect the panther from *them*. You know what will happen if they catch it. You saw what they did to the sea turtle."

Kiri pictured the magnificent sea turtle butchered on the beach. If Charro and the others caught the panther, they would probably kill it and sell it, and she didn't want that to happen. But what her da was doing didn't seem all that different to her. "What happens once you catch it?" she asked. "Aren't going to trade it to the wallers? Isn't that why they sent you all these supplies?"

"Yes," admitted her da. "Right now, the wallers are the only ones who can protect the panther. They'll keep it safe. They might even be able to breed it with similar sub-species. Preserving a species like this is worth more than anything the fugees could trade for it. It's worth more than the whole village, even, because once a species is lost, it's gone forever." He glanced at the sea-grape tunnels that led to the village. "We have to finish this fence."

Kiri looked back at the long web of razor-sharp wire separating the forest from the beach. The hot, claustrophobic feeling gnawed at her. It didn't feel right to divide the land like this. And it didn't feel right to trap the panther, either. It belonged here.

"Kiribati, if we don't get this fence up before the netters return, it's not just the panther that will be in danger."

Something about his voice unsettled Kiri. She searched her father's face, but he didn't smile or try to reassure her. Instead, he gave her a hard, steady look that sent chills down her spine.

All her life her da had tried to protect her from the harsh realities of where they lived. He'd shrugged off the risks of snakes, gators, fire ants, and scav attacks, dismissing every dangerous thing like it was just an obstacle in a game they could win if they were only clever enough. And so she'd learned to do the same, jumping gators and fire ant mounds, and nudging snakes aside with a stick. But now her da was doing the opposite, trying to get her to see the danger they were in.

If Charro and the others crossed before the fence could be completed, they wouldn't just scuffle with her da and spit words at him. Not after he'd shot at Senek. They'd attack and force both her and her da to leave. Or worse.

Instinctively, Kiri reached for the knife at her belt. Touching it gave her courage. She was careful to keep it hidden under her shirt, though. She didn't want her da to see the knife and ask how she'd gotten it.

"We need to be brave," said her da. "And we need to hurry. Can you do that for me?"

Kiri swallowed the sick feeling in her throat. She still didn't want to put up the fence, but what other choice did she have?

"Okay," she muttered.

"Good. Now stand back so I can activate the sections we've put up. That way, no one will stumble into the spider steel and get hurt." He pulled a palm-sized controller from his pack and entered a code into it.

Nothing about the sections they'd put up looked different to Kiri, but she heard a high, quiet hum. And when she reached toward the closest wire, the tiny hairs on her arm stood on end.

"Careful," said her da. "The field goes out on both sides."

He picked up a stick to demonstrate. As the end of the stick neared the spider steel, the buzzing increased and the air crackled. Martin jerked his hand back, dropping the stick. "See?" He clenched his fist and grimaced. "No one will be able to get close enough to touch the wires. Let's go. We've got five more spools to put up."

Kiri took the next spool and continued north, uncoiling wire around the cabbage palms and dead pines of the ghost forest. Some of the ruins were large and hard to navigate. Her da told her to stick to the beach side so as much land as possible could be included on their side.

When giving directions, Martin didn't sound at all like his normal, distracted self. Ever since he'd seen the paw print in the mud, he'd been more driven and decisive. He truly believed he was saving the panther.

It suddenly seemed clear to Kiri how people could be good and still be set against each other. Her da wasn't bad, and neither were the fugees. They just wanted different things. Her da wanted to catch the panther and send it to the wallers so it could be protected. And Charro and the other fugees wanted to trap the panther and sell it for food, medicine, fishing equipment, and other things that they needed to survive and protect their families. They were both trying to do what they believed was best.

*What about me?* thought Kiri. She didn't agree with the fugees or the wallers. *What do I want?*

She wanted to be able to run freely from the swamp to the beach. And she wanted to be welcome in the village again. She wanted to be whole, and not divided like she was now. Kiri recalled the sense of connection she'd felt when the panther had looked at her—a connection that had brought her mother back to her. She wanted to know her mother and feel that she belonged somewhere.

But all these wants seemed impossible now. Like the panther, she was trapped between two hostile sides while the space she had left to live in became smaller and smaller.

Kiri and her da worked deep into the night, until the fence stretched from the red mangroves to the south, up the edge of the ghost forest for miles, then inland to where the cypress swamp gave way to the mud lake.

"That should do it," said Martin once the wire was attached to the farthest power box and the last section had been activated. "Let's go home."

Kiri was so tired she could barely stand. Her da took her hand and lifted her over some of the mud pits and swamp channels on the way back to the stilt house. She couldn't wait to finally have some food and a bed to sleep in. But after what they'd done, severing the forest from the beach, she didn't think of it as her home anymore.

She didn't feel like she had a home anymore.

# PART II

*Devi of the Land*

# –9–

# A Plan

*It can't be true.*

That's what Kiri thought when she woke the next morning. The waller tridrone, her da shooting at the fugees, the fence cutting her off from the beach—it all had to be a nightmare.

But when she finally climbed out of bed and saw the mess of boxes and equipment in the main room of the stilt house, her hopes plummeted. An assortment of wires, spark panels, and vid eyes cluttered the kitchen counters and floor. Her da must have been awake for a while, setting up more equipment.

On the kitchen table sat a vid screen connected by a thick cord to a black box with several green and red lights on it.

Kiri turned on the screen. The image that came up was like a checkerboard. There were nine vid images, each showing different parts of the ghost forest or the swamp. Three of the images were labeled *Trap 1, Trap 2,* and *Trap 3*. The rest were simply given numbers from 1 to 6. Kiri realized the box connected to the vid screen must have been getting signals from different vid eyes out in the field. As she watched, her da moved across the image labeled *Trap 3*. He set palm fronds over a large metal cage to hide it from view.

She recognized the area where he was working. It was south, near the mangrove swamp. The other two traps looked to be farther north—one near where she'd encountered the panther, and the other by the northern ruins.

The thought of there being three panther traps already set up made her stomach quiver. Kiri turned off the vid screen and went to the rain basin for a glass of water. Then she dug through the food cabinet. There wasn't much to eat other than the bland waller powder her da got when he sold specimens to the city. She scooped out a cup, stirred it into her glass, and tried to gulp it down, but she was too upset to eat. She couldn't stop her thoughts from churning over what her da had done, and what she'd done by helping him.

Setting her breakfast aside, she grabbed a handful of palm nuts from the cabinet and climbed back to the loft to feed Snowflake. He cracked the nuts open and gingerly nibbled on the insides, not the least bit concerned about what had happened the night before or what might happen now.

"You're right, Snowflake," said Kiri. "No good will come from sitting here and worrying. I have to do something."

Snowflake cocked his head. He seemed perfectly content to sit inside all day and munch palm nuts. But when she pulled on her hoodie and started down the ladder, he dropped the nut he'd been chewing and hopped toward her. *Hold on,* he seemed to say. *You're not leaving me behind again.*

"You probably don't want to come with me," she told him. "Things could get bumpy."

Snowflake leaned off the edge by the ladder and nudged her hand, insistent.

"I know you're tough," she said. "It's just, everything's different now. We might not be able to get to the beach anymore, and if we're caught trying we could get in big trouble."

Snowflake stood on his hind legs and grabbed her shirt with his tiny paws. Kiri couldn't help smiling a little. "All right, you goof nut. You win. I'll take you with me."

She held open her hood and Snowflake climbed in. He snuffled loudly as he arranged a spot for himself.

Once outside, Kiri set off for the coast. Snowflake held on to her collar, looking over her shoulder like he normally did when they went to the beach. The little rat didn't seem the least bit worried about the fence, or fugees hating them, or Martin getting upset. His simple optimism spurred Kiri on and gave her hope. The more she walked, the better she felt.

"Things can't be that bad," she said. "You can't fence off the whole coast forever. There has to be a way to fix this. A way to make things go back to normal."

She kept chattering to Snowflake as she walked, until the beginnings of a plan took shape in her head—a vague outline for how she might get her da and the fugees to listen to her and get along again. It was risky, and her da would be furious if he found out what she planned on doing, but it seemed possible. She didn't think she could do it all alone, though, so she needed to find a way to cross the fence.

By the time Kiri reached the dead pines near the edge of the ghost forest, she was in a much better mood. From here, it wasn't very far to the sea-grape tunnels that led to the dunes, and once she reached the dunes, she'd be able to see the ocean waves breaking among the offshore tower ruins, same as always.

Kiri hurried toward the path. A high-pitched hum tickled her ears. Soon her skin prickled and her teeth buzzed, but she pressed on. Suddenly, the muscles in her legs convulsed. With a shout, she fell back.

Looking up, she glimpsed a thread of spider steel glistening in the late-morning light. The electric field around it must have repelled her. Kiri swallowed, determined to find a way across. She walked parallel to the fence for several hundred paces, but every time she approached the wire web her muscles twitched painfully and she had to move back. Even though the fence was barely visible, it felt as high and impenetrable as the walls surrounding a city.

The buzz of the fence started to give her a headache. Snowflake didn't seem to like it much, either. He turned frantically in her hood and shivered.

"Okay, okay," she said, when Snowflake started to squeak. "I won't walk into it again. But I'm not giving up."

She paced up and down the fence line. Every hundred yards or so, the nearly invisible metal threads went up to a black box nailed to the trunk of a tree. She wouldn't be able to get close to the boxes, though, without getting shocked.

Kiri noticed that her da had attached spark panels to some of the boxes. The panels hadn't been there the night before, so there must be a way to shut off the fence and reach them. She spied small black boxes strapped to the branches of a few trees too. They were probably some of the vid eyes sending images to the screen in their kitchen. Her da must have gotten up early to do all this. Or he hadn't slept.

It was on her third pass that Kiri spied a figure moving through the woods on the far side of the fence.

She crouched behind a cluster of saw palms, afraid of what might happen if a fugee spotted her. The figure stopped several feet from the fence and threw a stick at it, but the stick just bounced off the wire. Spider steel would cut through a whole tree before it snapped.

The figure continued north, parallel to the fence line.

That's when Kiri was able to make out the figure's skinny arms and floppy hair. Paulo!

She wanted to shout to him, but she stopped herself. What if other fugees were around and they heard? Besides, Paulo might hate her now. She'd feel worse than a gutted fish if he looked at her the way Senek had after her da shot at him.

Paulo was getting farther away and harder to see. Kiri's pulse skipped. This might be her only chance to talk to him. She picked up a rock and lobbed it over the fence.

The rock thumped to the ground a few feet behind Paulo. He paused and cocked his head.

Kiri threw another rock, only this time she made it land closer to the fence. Then she threw another and another, each time landing them closer to where she was hiding. Paulo took the hint and walked toward the saw palms.

He stopped abruptly, probably sensing the buzz of the fence. "Who's there?" he asked, staring at a thick curtain of kudzu vines.

Kiri threw another stone, but Paulo kept looking at the wrong area.

"Not there! Here!" she finally said, rustling some nearby saw palm leaves.

"Kiri?" Paulo stepped closer to where she was—or at least as close as he could get without being shocked by the fence. Then he glanced back at the sea-grape tunnels. There must have been others in the area. "Keep your voice down," he said, crouching low. He didn't sound angry or upset. Nervous, but not upset.

"I'm glad you're here," said Kiri.

Paulo shrugged. "I didn't believe it at first. I had to come see it for myself." He frowned at the fence. "This is bad, Kiri."

"I know."

"My da said your da tried to kill Senek," continued Paulo. "He's raging mad. Everyone in the village is."

"He didn't try to kill Senek," said Kiri. "He was just warning him to stay back." But she knew, even as she said it, that it made little difference. Her da had clearly threatened Senek. He'd threatened all the fugees by pointing the rifle at them, and by putting up the fence.

"Two fugees from the village walked into the fence this morning," said Paulo. "Tae walked into it, too. They all got shocked. Tae says his arm's still buzzing."

"They should have paid attention to the warning signs."

"They don't read," said Paulo. "Neither do I. You know that."

"The signs have pictures on them," replied Kiri, wondering why she was being so defensive. This wasn't how she thought talking to Paulo would go. Already, they were arguing. It was one thing to be stuck on different sides of a fence, and quite another to fight about it. "Anyhow, I don't want the fence to be here any more than you do," she said.

"Then why'd you help your da build it?"

"I didn't have a choice. Fugees were coming after us."

"Wallers always build fences," said Paulo. He sounded like his father.

"I'm not a waller. I'll never be a waller."

"The fence says otherwise."

Kiri bristled. "I hate it just as much as you do. Watch. I'll prove it."

"How?"

"You'll see." Kiri took a stick and carved the end into a flat wedge, like the tip of the screwdriver her da had used the night before when he'd set up the boxes. There must be an off switch. The only place she thought it could be was inside the hole at the top right corner.

Once she had the tip of the stick shaped right, Kiri reached toward the nearest box nailed to a tree. The buzzing intensified, making her teeth chatter and her hair stand on end. Snowflake squeaked and turned in her hood.

"All right, Snowflake, you baby." She reached into her hood and set the rat on the ground. Immediately, he scurried away from the fence. Then he sat back on his haunches and scratched his ears while watching Kiri out of the corner of one eye, as if he thought she was crazy.

"Nothing worth doing is ever easy," said Kiri. It was one of her da's favorite sayings—something he said before wading into muck or climbing a thorn tree to collect a specimen.

She pushed her tangled hair back and edged closer to the fence to try again with the stick.

Snowflake squeaked at her. "I'll be okay," she said, speaking to calm herself as much as him. She gritted her teeth and tried to poke the end of the stick into the hole in the black box. The buzzing shot up her arm and her muscles twitched uncontrollably. After a few seconds she had to drop the stick and jump back.

"You need gloves," said Paulo.

Kiri looked around. She didn't have gloves, but maybe something else would work.

Her sandals! The bottoms were thick tire rubber, and according to her da, rubber was a great spark stopper.

She slid her sandals off and tried to hold the stick with them. It was awkward and painful, but she finally managed to push the stick into the slot and turn it. With a faint click the buzzing stopped.

"Jumping jellies," said Paulo. "It's off."

"Just this section. The others are powered by different boxes," replied Kiri.

"Now what?" asked Paulo.

Kiri wanted to climb through the fence and run to the beach so she could see the waves and splash her toes in the water, but if any fugees spotted her, they'd know there was a break in the fence. She had to be patient. "Crawl under it before anyone sees," she said.

Paulo made a face. "Yeah, right."

"Trust me. I have a plan for how we can make things go back to normal. Now come on."

Paulo stared at the fence for several seconds, then he shrugged. "Devi Paulo to the rescue," he said in a goofy voice. He lay on his back and slid beneath the lowest strand of spider steel.

As soon as Paulo got clear of the fence on her side, Kiri rotated the stick, and the switch clicked back on. Immediately, the buzzing returned, and Kiri and Paulo jumped back.

"Huh, so this is how it looks over here," said Paulo, gazing about appreciatively. "Okay, I'm ready to go back."

"*Paulo . . .*"

"Kidding." He grinned. "But I really shouldn't stay long." Paulo glanced toward the sea-grape tunnels. "If someone sees me over here—"

"We just need to do one thing, then I'll turn off the fence and you can cross back."

"All right. So what's this 'one thing' we need to do?"

"Find the Shadow That Hunts."

"Very funny."

"I'm not joking," said Kiri. She scooped up Snowflake and set him on her shoulder. He nuzzled her hair for a moment before returning to her hood. "Let's go, before anyone sees you."

She set off into the ghost forest, away from the fence line. Paulo followed close behind, stepping clumsily. He'd explored a few of the ghost forest ruins with her in the past, but he didn't know his way around the woods nearly as well as Kiri did. She almost always went to the beach to see him. Traveling inland together was a new experience for both of them. Kiri had to stop several times to let Paulo catch up. Along the way, she explained why they needed to find the panther.

"Think about it," she said. "It's the reason all this has happened. My da put the fence up so he could trap the panther and send it to the wallers. And the netters are angry because they want to trap it and sell it to the boat people."

"So?"

"So *we* need to find the panther first," said Kiri. "If we can find it and keep both sides from trapping it, they'll listen to us. They'll have to, because they both want it."

"And then what?"

"Then we can make it so they're not fighting each other anymore. I'll get my da to promise not to trade the panther to the wallers, and I'll get the fugees to promise not to trap it and kill it. Then my da will take down the fence and everyone can get along again."

"Not all the fugees want to kill it, you know," said Paulo. "Some think it's a devi, like the Witch Woman said. She says it's wrong to trap it."

"Maybe it *is* a devi."

"You think so?" Paulo gave her a skeptical look.

Kiri shrugged. She didn't want to explain the connection she felt to the panther, or the strange way it had brought her mother to her. It all seemed too personal and crazy to admit. The more she thought about it, though, the more the marks on her shoulder and cheek tingled with wild energy. Devi marks.

"I think, whatever it is, we need to find it before anyone else does," she said.

Paulo bit his lip. "Say we do find it. What if it attacks us? It's probably hungry."

Kiri touched the wound on her shoulder. Not only was the panther much bigger than her, it was terrifyingly strong. She had no doubt it could end her life in an instant if it wanted to, only she wasn't about to tell Paulo this. She didn't want to scare him off. "It didn't kill me before," she said. "Besides, we're going to feed it. That way it'll know we're friendly and it won't hurt us."

"Feed it what?"

"Meat," said Kiri. "Fresh red waller meat. And I know exactly where to get some."

# -10-

## A Heart in the Ruins

"Ow!" yelled Paulo.

Kiri couldn't believe how ridiculously noisy he'd been, tromping through the ghost forest. "Shhh . . . ," she said. She had to giggle, though, when she saw him hopping around, doing a crazy dance while slapping his legs. "What on earth are you doing?"

"Something's stinging me!"

Kiri noticed a footprint, right in the middle of a fire ant mound. She was about to tell Paulo to grab some pine needles and rub them on his legs to brush off the ants when she noticed something else on the ground. "Paulo, stop jumping."

"I can't," he said. "They're everywhere!"

"Calm down and back up very slowly."

Paulo must have heard the fear in her voice, because he froze. Then he followed her gaze to a snake coiled in the dirt. The snake's tail shook, making a fast rattling sound, like an angry cicada.

"Snake!" said Paulo, jumping back onto the fire ant mound.

His sudden movement caused the snake to strike. Luckily, it was a small diamondback and couldn't reach Paulo's leg. But Kiri saw two more diamondbacks coiled in the grass nearby. If Paulo started jumping again, he'd get bit for sure.

She grabbed a stick off the forest floor and used it to scoot the nearest snake away, right as Paulo yelped from the second round of fire ant stings. He stumbled toward her, frantically slapping his legs, eyes wide with fear.

"Sorry, little one," said Kiri to the snake, hoping she hadn't hurt it. She'd relocated diamondbacks dozens of times before, and she could usually pick them up with a stick and set them aside without them even coiling. They were generally calm and lazy, but Paulo's spastic movements had upset them.

"Did you just apologize to the snake?" Paulo asked.

"Yes. It was sitting there, basking in the sun, when you almost stepped on it. It could have died."

Paulo shook his head. "*I* could have died."

"Maybe," said Kiri. "But diamondbacks hate to bite people. It's a waste of venom."

"Snakes are a waste of venom."

Snowflake chittered from Kiri's hood, agreeing with Paulo's sentiments about snakes.

Paulo sat on a log a good distance from the snakes and fire ants. He took off his sandals and counted twenty-one red welts on his legs. "I think I'll name them all," he said. "That's Stinger, and Red Rage, and Freckle Beast . . ."

Kiri groaned. "If you soak your legs in a tide pool when you get home it will take some of the sting away," she said. "Now, let's go. We have to find the Shadow That Hunts."

Paulo shot her a strange look. His brow knotted as he put his sandals back on. He glanced around the forest warily.

"What?" asked Kiri.

"Nothing," he said. "Just, why do you call it the Shadow That Hunts instead of a panther, like your da?"

"It means the same thing, doesn't it?"

"No," said Paulo. "If it's the Shadow That Hunts, then we shouldn't even be out here trying to find it."

Kiri studied him. Usually Paulo was full of jokes and mischief, always making goofy faces and saying funny things. A lot of kids considered him weak because he was small and skinny, but Kiri knew it took courage to make others laugh. He was loyal, too, and honest, and not afraid of getting in trouble to help a friend. No one else in the village would have dared to cross the fence to search with her, even if she asked them to, which she wouldn't. Paulo was braver than almost anyone she knew, so it took her a moment to realize that he was truly frightened. "I'll make sure to avoid any snakes and fire ants," she said. "You just have to step where I do."

Paulo snapped off a branch nearby. "It's not that."

"Then what?"

He sighed and thumped the branch against the log. "The Shadow That Hunts is another name for death. People in the village are saying that you've been marked by death. And they say that whatever death marks, it always returns to claim."

"If it comes to claim me, then it will be easy to find. Right?" replied Kiri, hoping to lighten the mood.

"I don't want death to claim you," said Paulo. He nodded to her shoulder. "That doesn't look good."

"It's just a scratch." Kiri pulled her shirt over the red marks on her shoulder. "It'll heal."

"Do wallers believe in devi?"

"Why are you asking *me* that? I've never even been to a waller city."

"Tae says the wallers used to have gods, but they stopped believing in them. So their gods got angry and left, and that's why they hide behind walls. They're afraid of everything because they don't have gods anymore."

"I don't know what wallers believe," Kiri said. "Maybe they believe *they're* the gods."

"Is that what your da believes?"

"Who knows? He never talks about stuff like that. He

just talks about specimens—things he can study and capture and preserve."

"Typical waller."

A rush of anger made Kiri's brow knot. "What's that supposed to mean?"

"You know . . ." Paulo looked back through the woods toward where the fence was. "Wallers like to put things in jars and boxes, right? They like to separate things and control them. That's how they are. It's what they do."

"And fugees are better?" countered Kiri. "They catch things and kill them—like that sea turtle your da killed."

"That's different," Paulo said. "Fugees only kill to eat, and they make what they eat a part of them. They don't separate themselves from everything else. They take and give and share. Like the sea turtle: my da tried to share it with your da. He even would have shared it with other sea turtles if any had come by," he added with a goofy grin.

The ridiculous image of turtles lining up to eat turtle soup caught Kiri off guard, and she laughed. Just like that, her anger faded.

She headed north, toward the area in the ruins where her da had set up one of his traps. Paulo followed, careful to step where Kiri did this time. "What about you?" she asked after a few minutes. "What do you believe?"

Paulo didn't answer at first. Kiri glanced back and saw him staring at the stick he carried, as if the answer might be in the twisted grains of wood. "I believe the gods are still here, only they're broken into little pieces now. And some of those pieces might be devi, like the Shadow That

Hunts." He scooped up a pinecone, tossed it into the air, and tried to hit it with the stick, but missed.

"You think some sort of god piece scratched me?"

"It wasn't a feral cat that did it. Or if it was, then it must have been the god of all feral cats." Paulo picked up another pinecone. This time he managed to hit it a little ways. "Anyhow, the Witch Woman says that when three devi mark someone, you have to listen to them because they've been chosen by the Wise One to speak. She's telling everyone that you've been marked by two devi already—one from the water, and one from the land."

"So what happens if I'm marked by a third?"

"Who knows? Then I'd have to listen to you, I guess."

"So I could tell you to eat sand and you would?"

Paulo mimicked gulping down a spoonful of sand. "Yum!" He smiled, but he still seemed anxious. "Things in the village are different now, Kiri. People are hungry, and angry about the fence. They're saying a lot of stuff."

"Like what?"

He shrugged. "Stuff about wallers taking everything and ruining everything. I know you're not like that, but not everyone knows you like I do. Just be careful, okay? I don't want anything to happen to you."

🐢

Kiri spotted the vid eye first—a small black cube strapped to the branches of a pine with a thin antenna sticking up.

"Wait!" She tugged at Paulo's shirt, pulling him back.

Luckily, the glass lens seemed to be pointed the other way, at the crumbling ruin that Kiri had seen on the vid screen that morning.

They crept up to the base of the tree. From there, Kiri could see what the vid eye was watching. Only a corner of the concrete ruin remained, and it was mostly covered in kudzu vines. Against this green-and-white backdrop a thick cut of red meat dangled from a strap. It looked odd, hanging there in the open, until Kiri tilted her head and spotted a glint of sunlight off a thread of spider steel.

The more she looked, the more she could make out the spider steel mesh and rods that formed the trap. Her da had done a good job hiding the walls of the trap beneath kudzu vines and Spanish moss, but Kiri could tell that if something tugged on the hanging meat, the open side would snap down, closing the rectangular box.

She cut a long palm frond with her knife and handed it to Paulo. He looked confused until she pantomimed climbing the tree and covering the vid eye with the palm leaves. "Gently," Kiri whispered to him. "Try to make it look like a leaf fell in front of the lens."

Paulo scampered up the lower branches and leaned out, holding on with only one hand while swinging the palm branch in front of the lens with the other.

Once the vid eye's view was blocked, Kiri went to investigate the trap. The dangling meat looked thick and fresh. Kiri recalled seeing packages of red meat in some of the cold boxes the wallers had sent in the tridrone. Her stomach rumbled as she stared at it. They never got to eat meat like this. She would have traded a bucketful of sand fleas just to taste a bite.

Snowflake took advantage of her stillness to climb onto her shoulder. His nose twitched as he sniffed the air and caught a whiff of the meat.

"Careful," she whispered, more to herself than Snowflake. If she got too close, the sliding wall of the trap might catch her when it closed. She worked a stick through the wire mesh and snagged the meat with it. Then she gently swung the meat closer to the open side, being careful not to tug it. Pull too hard, and the trap would shut.

After several tries, she managed to swing the meat close enough that she could grab it with two fingers.

Paulo whistled impatiently, but Kiri ignored him. If she could get her knife out, she might be able to cut the strap that held the meat without setting off the trap.

Paulo whistled again, louder this time.

Kiri finally looked over. He was leaning far out from the tree, trying to keep the palm frond in front of the vid eye with one shaking arm while attempting to blow a fly away from his face. His hair kept going up and down with every puff of breath, but the fly continued to buzz around him. *Hurry!* his eyes seemed to say.

Several things happened at once. Snowflake scampered down Kiri's arm to get a taste of the meat and Kiri jerked her hand back the tiniest bit.

*Snap!*

The door of the wire cage slid shut. Then Paulo started to fall, uncovering the vid eye as he went.

Quickly, Kiri rolled away from the cage until she was beyond the vid eye's view.

Snowflake bounded toward her, spooked by the quick *snap* of the trap. He scurried into her hands and nuzzled her fingers to calm himself.

"There was a fly," said Paulo.

Kiri glared at him.

"It was a big fly," he added.

"Let's go before my da finds us." She kissed Snowflake on his head and returned him to her hood. The little rat shivered. "Even if the vid eye didn't see me, my da will know the trap's been sprung."

They ran as fast as they could toward the fence.

"Did you get it?" asked Paulo once they stopped to rest.

Kiri held up the cut of meat she'd pulled free. "Clever as a crab."

Paulo's eyes widened and a grin dimpled his cheeks. "Nice! Devi Paulo wants some!"

"It's not for us. Or rats," she added when Snowflake climbed onto her shoulder.

"Pretty please? Just a tiny bite? I'm starving."

Kiri considered cutting off some of the thick, juicy meat she held. They'd have to cook it first, and that would mean a fire. . . .

*"Paul-ooo!"* called a distant voice.

Paulo's smile fell. He crouched behind a bush.

"Paulo! You better come home right now!"

"It's Tae," whispered Paulo. "My ma probably sent him to find me."

Kiri checked the sky. The sun was already setting. Several hours had passed since Paulo crossed over.

"I should go. My da must be back from fishing."

"Give me a minute," said Kiri.

She jogged to a patch of sandy ground between two pine trees. It wasn't very far from where the tracks she'd seen the other night had led. One of the nearby pines was still alive, even though kudzu vines covered most of it. Kiri cut off a long vine and tied one end around the meat. She looped the vine over a branch so the meat dangled about four feet off the ground, where pythons and rats wouldn't be able to reach it.

"Why'd you do that?" asked Paulo, practically drooling as he stared at the meat dangling from the end of the vine.

"It's an offering for the Shadow That Hunts, so it knows we're friends."

"You're just going to leave it there?"

"Yep. It's the perfect place," said Kiri. If the panther came for the meat, it would leave tracks in the sandy ground that she could follow. And this way, the panther wouldn't be lured by hunger into one of her da's traps.

"Paulo!" Tae called again. "I swear if you don't get your butt over here, I'm going to rub your face in fish guts!"

"It's always fish guts with him," said Paulo. "Never bird poop or sea slugs. Help me cross back?"

Kiri took one last look at the offering she'd left before jogging with Paulo to the fence. The meat swayed in a breeze above the sandy ground—a dark red heart among the ruins.

# —11—

# Kiri's Secret

That night Kiri couldn't sleep. Despite how tired she felt, every time she closed her eyes, her head spun and her shoulder itched.

She did her best not to toss and turn. Earlier in the evening, when she'd become dizzy and stumbled on her way up to the sleeping loft, her da had fussed over her. He inspected the wound on her shoulder and put some cream on it, but as far as Kiri could tell, the cream didn't help. The scratches were still puffy and red, and the surrounding skin felt warm and red too, like a sunburn.

Da took her temperature with the same thermometer Kiri used to test the temperature of the waves. The metal rod tasted salty from the ocean. After checking it twice, her da recorded her temperature in his logbook. "You need to stay in bed," he told her. "Get plenty of rest. I don't want you going out at all tomorrow, Kiribati."

Kiri closed her eyes and tried to fall asleep, but real sleep wouldn't come. She dozed in a restless way, listening to the sounds of her da working in the room below. He put together some more equipment and left—probably to reset the trap she'd sprung. He hadn't scolded her for setting off the trap or taking the meat, so Kiri figured she hadn't been spotted by the vid eye. Her da must have thought a rat or a python or some other small animal had stolen the meat.

Around midnight, Martin finally returned and climbed to the loft to get some sleep. Kiri was delirious with thirst. For the past hour or so she'd felt like she was floating near the ceiling, not entirely connected to her body anymore. She wanted to get a drink and clear her head, but she didn't want her da to know she was still awake. As soon as she thought about moving, though, the marks on her shoulder and cheek began to itch again. Or rather, the sensation started as an itch, then became a hot, prickling tingle, like a thousand tiny crabs pinching her, urging her to move.

She shut her eyes and tried to focus on other things. Images of the ghost forest scrolled through her head, almost as if she were sprinting through the woods. She pictured herself running along the fence line, desperate to find a way to cross so she could get to the coast. Then she turned inland and darted through the underbrush, barely making a sound until she reached the dark cypress ponds in the swamp. Leaning over the edge of the pond to drink, she saw her reflection in the moonlight. Only it wasn't *her* reflection. Two fiery green eyes blinked back at her, set in a round, fur-covered face.

Panther eyes.

*Panthers hunt at night.*

Kiri startled awake. She was in her bed again, but she didn't feel completely there anymore. The tingling prickle of the devi marks kept urging her to move. She pushed off the blankets and crawled to the ladder.

Snowflake was sound asleep in his nest. Kiri decided not to wake him. The poor little rat would never willingly leave her, but he was probably worn out from getting bounced around in her hood all day. She wasn't sure how much more he could take.

She hurried down the ladder and out of the stilt house, just like she'd done the other night, only quieter this time—swift as a panther prowling through the forest.

Kiri ran to the ghost forest, avoiding all the areas she'd seen on her da's screen where the vid eyes must be. Then she continued north, toward the jagged concrete ruins, to check on the meat she'd hung.

It was gone.

She studied the sandy ground. The nearly full moon shone bright enough that she could make out several round divots in the soft earth. Panther tracks.

Kiri circled the area like her da had taught her to do, being careful not to step on the trail as she determined which direction the panther had gone. Animals sometimes doubled back, but this time the trail seemed clear. She followed the tracks north, deeper into the ghost forest.

After a while, she didn't need to see the tracks to know which way the panther had gone. Maybe it was the lay of the land or the subtle broken-leaf and matted-earth signs of an animal path, but following the trail became easier.

The pines of the ghost forest gave way to a marl grass clearing. Thick stands of saw palm bushes clustered beneath a few fallen trees at one edge. Kiri headed toward the palm bushes but stopped halfway, sensing that she was being watched.

She scanned the area. Something moved through the tall grass ahead of her. It took a few steps, then paused, then took a few steps again, as if trying to sneak up on her.

Kiri froze. The devi marks on her shoulder and cheek tingled, and her heart beat madly, but she forced herself to stay still. Whatever stalked her seemed clumsier than the panther had been. She caught a glimpse of its ears in the silvery moonlight—two triangles on top of its head, only smaller than the panther's and lower to the ground. Much lower.

The creature charged and leapt at her foot. Kiri startled back. The creature hopped back as well, but Kiri could see it clearly now.

It was a cub! A fluffy, spotted panther cub!

The cub darted into the tall grass where it had come from.

"It's okay," whispered Kiri. She crouched so as not to appear intimidating. "I won't hurt you."

The cub pounced again, taking a ridiculously high leap and landing a few feet in front of her, like a cricket. Then it hopped back, disappearing into the grass.

Kiri giggled. She knew the cub was trying to look fierce, but its clumsy high hops were so funny she couldn't stop herself from laughing. "You're just a little cricket, aren't you?"

This time, the panther cub tried to sneak around her. Kiri heard the grass rustle, but she didn't turn. Most animals felt threatened when stared at. If she looked away and was patient, even shy animals sometimes came up to her.

The cub stalked closer. Kiri felt its fur brush her bare calf. The unexpected touch sent a shiver through her.

"That's right," she whispered. "I'm a friend."

The cub batted the fraying ends of her hoodie. Its claws got stuck in the fabric and it rolled back, twisting and tugging frantically to free its paw.

"Calm down, silly," whispered Kiri as she unhooked its claws. From a glimpse of its belly she could tell it was a boy cub. He scampered off into the tall grass, then lowered his chin to his paws and studied her.

Unlike the mother panther, the cub's coat was speckled with black markings. He also had more black on his face and around the tips of his ears. And his eyes, instead of being yellow green, looked light blue, although it was hard to tell for certain in the moonlight. His paws were comically large for his short legs. Despite how fierce he tried to appear, his fluffy fur made him resemble a speckled puffball.

Kiri stretched her hand out toward the cub. "What are you doing here?" she asked. "Where's your ma?"

The cub stalked forward, sniffed her hand, then hopped back and turned a frantic circle in the grass, as if startled by his own tail.

Kiri grinned. She kept her hand out, careful not to do anything that might scare the cub away. The next time he approached, he nudged her palm, then flopped onto his back, letting her pet his white belly while he batted her hand with soft paws.

"Are you lost?" she whispered. "Did you lose your ma?"

The cub darted into the grass, only to circle back a moment later and nudge her hand again.

"I lost my ma, too," she said.

The cub purred as he pressed his head into Kiri's palm, nuzzling her anytime she stopped petting him.

Something else stirred the grass. Kiri looked up. Another fluffy face with blue eyes peered out at her from the shadows. This cub had a dark line across its muzzle, like a mustache. A third cub poked through the grass, next to the other. As soon as it saw her, it turned and skittered into a gap in the saw palms.

"Three of you?" whispered Kiri.

The cub she'd named Cricket batted her hand, urging her to pet him again. She stroked his belly some more, while the one with the mustache yawned and licked its paws. Suddenly, both Cricket and Mustache turned and darted into the gap in the saw palms.

Kiri crouched a few feet from the prickly palm bushes.

"It's all right," she whispered. "I won't hurt you. I'm your friend."

One by one, the three cubs scampered out. First came Cricket, hopping and turning quick little circles before rubbing against her legs. Then Mustache, flopping on the ground at the edge of the saw palms and yawning. And finally Skitter—that's what Kiri decided to call the skittish one who'd run off.

She petted Cricket with one hand while holding her other hand out until both Mustache and Skitter edged close enough to sniff her fingers. Every time Kiri moved, Skitter bolted back to the shelter of the dense saw palm bushes.

*It's a den!* thought Kiri.

Her muscles tensed as she realized what this meant. Gators in the swamp would snap at anything that approached their nests. And fire ants would sting anything that stepped near their mounds. Even rats, squirrels, and mice would fiercely protect their dens. So if the mother panther caught her here, she might attack.

Kiri scanned the clearing. The tall grass field and surrounding forest seemed incredibly still except for the cubs. Then, on a thick branch above the den, Kiri saw a long, snakelike shape ripple in the darkness.

Her breath caught. Kiri followed the undulating, snakelike silhouette of a tail to a muscular form crouched on the branch. The panther mother was perched less than ten feet away, ready to pounce.

As if sensing Kiri's gaze, the panther raised her head and focused her fiery green eyes on Kiri.

Kiri didn't dare move. She didn't even blink as she held the panther's gaze, just as she'd done the other night.

The panther had been there all along, watching her.

*She allowed me to approach,* thought Kiri. *She let me play with the cubs.*

The space between each heartbeat grew as thick as storm clouds rolling in. Then the panther mother lowered her head onto the branch and closed her eyes. With that one simple gesture, the storm clouds passed.

Cricket went back to batting Kiri's hoodie and tugging at the torn cloth, while Mustache yawned and Skitter ran quick little circles around Kiri's legs. And Kiri went back to playing with the cubs, yet everything felt different. Kiri's devi marks tingled, only instead of prickles of restless energy, they filled her with a warm sense of belonging. The panthers had accepted her.

She couldn't say how long she stayed there, playing with the cubs. Time didn't seem to have the same meaning anymore. Still, when the sky began to lighten, Kiri knew she had to go back. If her da discovered her missing and tracked her to the den, he might try to capture the cubs and send them to the wallers. They'd be taken from here, and it would be her fault.

And if her da or the fugees trapped the mother panther, the cubs would starve.

Fixing things between her da and the fugees had just gotten a whole lot more complicated. But more than ever, Kiri knew what she had to do.

She had to protect the panthers.

# –12–

## A Break in the Fence

"I have a secret," whispered Kiri.

It was late in the day when she finally found Paulo. She'd slept through most of the morning and some of the afternoon and her muscles still ached, but the thought of the cubs and all that had happened the night before energized her. "It's a really good secret."

Paulo crouched among the saw palms on the other side of the fence. He tugged at his shirt and shifted from foot to foot. "I can't cross today. You should go home. Stay in your house—"

"The offering we put out is gone," said Kiri. "Something amazing happened. You have to cross."

"I can't," repeated Paulo, twisting his shirt tight.

"Of course you can. I'll switch off the fence like before,

then you can slide under and we can steal the meat from the trap again."

"You shouldn't be here."

"We have to hurry. I saw my da on the vid screen. He's down near the red mangrove swamp right now, checking the fence. If we go quickly, we can steal the meat from all three traps. That way the panther won't get caught." Kiri tried to switch off the black box with the stick. The electric field made her arms numb and her teeth vibrate, but she pushed through it.

"I'm not coming across today," said Paulo.

"Please? It won't take long. You just have to climb the tree and cover the vid eye like before." At last, she worked the end of the stick into the hole on the box. Once it was firmly in, she released the end of the stick and jerked her hand back. The stick stayed in the box, waiting for her to turn it.

"You shouldn't be here, Kiri," Paulo said. "The only reason I came is to tell you I'm not crossing so you'd stop looking for me."

"Why? Did you get in trouble?" Kiri figured that must be why Paulo was acting so weird. "It won't be like yesterday, I promise—no more snakes or fire ants. How are Freckle Beast and Red Rage anyway?"

"They're fine." Paulo rubbed the stings on his leg, but he still seemed nervous. "Just forget all this. Go back to the swamp."

"No way. There's too much to do." Kiri reached up to turn the stick. "Help me steal the meat. Then, if you promise to never, ever tell anyone, I'll tell you my secret. Or part of it, at least. It's the most amazing thing. Trust me, you won't regret—"

"Regret what?" asked Tae, crashing through the saw palms behind Paulo. "Regret betraying us?"

"Tae! Quiet!" hissed Paulo.

"They're over here!" called Tae.

Akash forced his way into the clearing on the other side of the fence from Kiri. She pulled the stick out of the box and stepped back, but Tae had already seen her, so there was no point in running. And anyway, the fence was still on. The fugees couldn't cross it.

"Liar," said Tae, glaring at his brother. "I knew you'd gone across. Now go get Da. Tell him we found a way through the fence."

"No," said Paulo.

"Go," repeated Tae, shoving his brother. "Get him or I'll make you wish you had."

Paulo still didn't move.

"Fine. I'll get him myself," said Tae.

"Don't! You can't tell him."

"Who's going to stop me?" Tae turned to go.

Paulo tackled him. Palm fronds snapped and crunched as the two brothers fell wrestling to the ground.

Paulo fought hard, but he couldn't keep his older brother down for long. Pretty soon Tae had him in a head-lock.

"Traitor," growled Tae. "You know what happens to traitors?"

Paulo's face turned red and his eyes bulged.

"Let him go!" yelled Kiri from the other side of the fence.

Tae kept squeezing his brother. Kiri had to do something to help Paulo. She tried hitting Tae with the stick, but the fence kept shocking her. Using the stick's carved end, she reached toward the black box again. If she could just switch off the fence for a second, she could make Tae let Paulo go.

Paulo squirmed, moving closer to the buzzing wires.

Tae yelled and released his hold on Paulo. He rolled back from the fence, grabbing his ear. A wire must have shocked him.

Paulo scrambled back as well. "Kiri, run!"

But Kiri didn't leave. She didn't want anything bad to happen to Paulo because of her.

Heavy footsteps crashed through the ghost forest. Akash must have slipped off to get others the moment Tae and Paulo had started fighting. A metallic taste coated Kiri's tongue as palm fronds on the far side of the fence shook and fell. Someone was chopping through the bushes with a machete.

"There she is." Senek thrust his sunburned, sweaty face into the clearing. He swung a rusty machete, slicing a bigger opening in the brush.

"Told you my boys would suss her out," said Charro, stepping through the branches behind Senek. His eyes narrowed on Kiri. "Hello, Waller Girl. You going to let us through?"

Kiri shook her head. "I can't."

"She's lying," said Tae. He pointed to a nearby tree. "There's a box on the other side. It's a switch or something. She was reaching for it with a stick."

"Switch off the fence, girl," said Charro. "Then we can all be friends again."

Snowflake peeked out of Kiri's hood and chuffed protectively.

"Well, look at that. You brought your pet," said Charro. "He's a cute one, isn't he?"

Kiri tried to shoo Snowflake back into her hood. She didn't trust Charro's compliments.

"You always did have a way with animals. It's quite something. Don't you think it's something, Senek?"

"Yeah," said Senek. "She's got a gift."

"She does. With a gift like that, you could be a great netter, like me," said Charro. "See, I know you understand things more than your da. You know this fence can't stay here. It's not right to keep us cut off from the forest like this. You hold the key. Let us through and all will be forgiven."

The metallic taste in Kiri's mouth grew stronger, making her want to spit. "No," she said. "You'll kill the panther."

"That panther doesn't belong to your da or the wallers," replied Charro. "It's ours, and we need it. People are hungry, Kiri. Trading that panther will bring food to the village. It will mean life for a lot of us. Help us catch it and you'll be a hero to the whole village."

Kiri's gaze fell to the thick metal rod Charro carried.

She thought it might be some kind of walking stick or club. Then she realized it was something much worse. "Where'd you get that?"

"This?" said Charro, lifting the rusty long gun. "This is what I traded the rest of the sea turtle for. It's what makes us equals with your da. Now, I'm going to ask nicely one more time. Will you turn off the fence so we can all be friends again? Or do I need to use this?"

"Kiri run!" shouted Paulo. He threw a handful of sand in his father's face.

"Dang it, boy!" snapped Charro. "Whose side are you on?"

Kiri took off while the netter was distracted.

"Get back here, Waller Girl!" shouted Senek, but Kiri didn't slow.

*BOOM!*

The sound slammed her ears, loud as lightning striking too close. She dove to the ground and crawled behind a thick stand of inkberry bushes.

Glancing back, she saw Charro still had the long gun raised, only he wasn't aiming at her. Instead, he aimed at the tree where the black box hung. The first shot had taken out a chunk of bark, exposing the raw yellow wood underneath.

*BOOM!*
*BOOM!*

The third shot blew the box completely off the tree.

With a flash of sparks and a shattering of plastic, the section of the fence went dead.

# —13—

## A Lucky Turn

Charro called for Kiri to come back. He sent Tae and Akash after her, but Kiri kept running. No one knew this area as well as she did. She took all the quick cuts she could through the swamp. The fugees, armed with machetes and a gun, were sure to cross the fence and hunt the panther. They'd hunt her da, too, if they found him. She had to warn him.

Dizziness swarmed her body. She stumbled, feeling delirious, but she couldn't rest. Not now. Snowflake clung to her collar, chittering to her every time she slowed.

Kiri shouted for her da as she neared the stilt house, but there was no response. Ducking inside, she saw that the waller rifle and his pack were gone. Why wasn't he here? He must still be out in the field somewhere. All he cared about was catching the panther.

She checked the vid screen set up in the kitchen. At first she saw only trees, grass, and vines on the screen. Then, in one vid square, she spotted Charro and Senek making their way through a stretch of tall grass.

Kiri recognized the field. It stood between the ghost forest and the swamp, on *this* side of the fence. Fear coiled in her chest, tightening like a python with every breath. They weren't that far from the house. She grabbed a water bottle and some energy powder, along with a handful of palm nuts, which she dropped into her hood for Snow-flake.

The rat poked his head up and sniffed. After a day of commotion, he probably wanted to curl up in the loft and sleep.

"It's not safe here, Snowflake," Kiri said. "Not any-more. We have to leave."

She scratched behind his ears to comfort him until he ducked back into her hood. Then she gave the house one last look, not sure if she'd ever be able to return.

Once outside, Kiri considered shouting for her da. Then she thought better of it. Who knew how many fugees had crossed the fence by now? If any heard her, they'd come running. Her hand went to the worn handle of her mother's knife hanging from her belt. "Help me find him," she whispered.

It was almost sunset. That's when predators like the panther usually ventured out to hunt. Her da had probably gone to observe the trap she'd set off the other day. He'd find a high spot where he could keep watch from a distance. There weren't many hills in the area, but there were some ruins that still had three or four floors aboveground.

It took Kiri almost an hour to reach the ruins because she had to take the long way around to avoid Charro and the others. And because her legs felt jittery and weak. Something was wrong with her, but she couldn't dwell on that. She needed to stay focused on finding her da before the fugees did.

At last, she spotted her da high up in a live oak tree, adjusting a vid eye.

"They're coming!" she said.

Martin climbed down immediately. "What are you doing here, Kiribati? You're supposed to be in bed. You need to rest."

"They shot one of the boxes and crossed," said Kiri. "I saw them on the vid screen."

"Where?"

Kiri told him about spotting Charro and the others in the field on this side of the fence. She told him about Charro's long gun, too.

"You okay?" asked her da.

She nodded and said she was fine, but that didn't stop Martin from feeling her forehead and fussing over her.

Then his gaze flicked to the knife at her belt. She hadn't realized she was still holding it.

"That knife . . . let me see it."

Kiri held the knife up, reluctant to let it go.

Martin studied the fish and other designs etched into the metal blade. "This was your mother's knife. How'd you get this?"

*She gave it to me,* thought Kiri, but she couldn't say that out loud. Rationally, she knew her dead mother couldn't have given her the knife. The Witch Woman must have stitched the sheath to her belt while she'd slept. Nevertheless, the vision she'd had of her mother felt true. Her ma was looking out for her—the knife seemed proof of that. "It was a gift," said Kiri, sliding the knife back into the sheath.

Martin looked like he was about to question her further, but a beeping sound interrupted him. He pulled his vid pad from his pocket and checked the message on the screen. "Trap one's been triggered."

"By what?"

"I'm not sure." He continued studying the small screen.

"Did someone steal the meat?" she asked, wondering if Paulo had crossed back as well. Maybe he'd gone to the trap to get a taste of the meat.

"No. It's the panther. We caught it!"

Her da grabbed his pack and set off for the trap. "We're lucky, Kiribati. Things might work out after all."

# –14–

## The Truth at Last

They slowed as they neared the trap, approaching from the downwind side. The wire door had snapped shut and a small red light on top blinked, but all Kiri saw inside were leaves, grass, and shadows. The meat was gone, only the hanging strap remained. Then a shadow among the leaves moved.

The Shadow That Hunts.

The panther raised her head and stared at them. Kiri held her gaze, but the panther's fiery green eyes weren't welcoming now. The creature in the cage bared her teeth and made a high hissing sound—her tan-colored ears pressed flat against her skull in a threatening posture. Snowflake shivered in Kiri's hood.

Martin signaled for Kiri to stay back. Suddenly the panther leapt at him. She hit the side of the cage and was thrown back to the ground by the wires and bars, but the panther didn't stop. Quick as a blink, she rolled to her paws and threw herself against the mesh walls again and again. The cage still didn't give. After the fourth or fifth attempt, the panther slumped to the ground, eyelids drooping. She hissed at Martin, but she sounded weaker this time. One side of her mouth sagged.

"What's wrong with her?" asked Kiri.

"I put a tranquilizer in the meat in case the trap malfunctioned again."

So that's what her da thought had happened the other day.

"What a specimen!" continued her da. "I can't believe it." He unslung his pack and dug in the front pocket, pulling out a plastic bag with an old waller book in it. Then he flipped through the book, tearing a couple of pages in his haste, until he got to the entry he sought. He looked up, comparing the panther to the description in the book. "It really is *Puma concolor*," he said. "These haven't been seen in decades. I thought I'd imagined the prints, or someone had released a hybrid. But it has to be *Puma concolor* . . ."

He kept muttering to himself as he crept forward, talking about how the panther appeared to be female and starving—that's why it had gone after the meat. It still looked healthy, if a bit on the thin side.

The panther closed her eyes and panted heavily.

Seeing her in the cage made Kiri feel gutted and empty. By trapping and drugging the panther, her da had taken a wild, awe-inspiring creature and turned it into something small and angry. A panther in a cage was no more a panther than water in a bucket was the ocean.

"The satphone!" said Martin. "I left it at the house to charge. It's the only way to contact my patrons."

Kiri slumped against a tree, careful not to squish Snowflake. The little rat clambered onto her good shoulder and groomed the hair by her ear, but she paid him no mind. How could her da do this? Why was he so fixated on calling the wallers and trading the panther?

"Kiribati, are you listening?" he asked. "I need to leave you for a little bit."

She shook her head, unable to shake the sense that she was missing something important.

"Stay here. I'll run back to the house to get the satphone," said her da.

"Why?"

"To contact my patrons."

*What about me?* she wanted to say, but she didn't. All he cared about was trading the panther.

"Rest until I return," he said. "Don't go anywhere. And don't step near that trap. Even if the panther looks asleep, it's still incredibly dangerous. Understand?"

"No," said Kiri. The sense that she was missing something important kept nagging at her.

"I have to get the satphone, Kiribati. You just need

to be strong a little longer, and then you'll get better. I promise."

*"Better?"* she whispered the word, but she couldn't make it fit with what was going on. How would getting the satphone make her better? If her da had the phone, he'd call the wallers and they'd take the panther away. She shivered, despite how hot she felt.

Martin knelt beside her and pressed his hand to her forehead like he used to do when she was little and not feeling well. With his touch, cool against her sweating skin, she suddenly saw the truth.

"I'm sick, aren't I?" she said. "And not just a little sick. It's the fever Charro talked about. The scratch got infected and now I'm going to die. Like Ma died."

Her da winced. For a split second he looked lost, then his expression hardened. "You're *not* going to die. Once I have the satphone I can get you medicine that will make you better."

"That's what you were looking for in the tridrone," continued Kiri, piecing together the other things that hadn't made sense before. "You asked the wallers to send medicine because the scratch looked bad. But they didn't."

"They will now," said her da. "For the panther, they'll take you in and treat you. I'll make sure of it."

*For the panther,* thought Kiri. Her da wanted to trade the panther to save her life.

"What about the fugees?" she asked.

Her da glanced around, as if he thought they might be close. Then his gaze settled on the vid eye he'd placed in a nearby tree. He climbed the tree and tore the cube off the branch.

"There," he said. "Now, even if the fugees get into our house, they won't know you're here. Or the panther. They won't find either of you. Just be brave a little longer while I get the satphone." He leaned down and kissed her forehead. "I won't lose you, Kiribati. You mean more than the world to me, and I'm not going to let what happened to your mother happen to you. I swear it."

Kiri closed her eyes, letting his words sink in. Her mother had been sick like this, too, and the wallers could have saved her, but they didn't. So Charro blamed her da for Laria's death. If only her da had persuaded the wallers to give her ma medicine, she'd still be alive. No wonder her da was so obsessed with catching the panther. He needed something big—something the wallers would be willing to trade a lot for—to save her.

*But what about the cubs?* thought Kiri. *If the wallers take the panther, what will happen to the cubs? Without a mother, they'll die.*

Kiri suddenly remembered that her da didn't know about the cubs. He thought there was only one panther at stake. Not four. She opened her eyes and started to tell him, but he was gone. There was just his pack, sitting by the tree where she lay. She called for him, only it did no good. Her voice sounded weak and he must have already been too far away to hear.

*You have to give something to get something,* she

thought. *That's how it works with wallers.* So how much would she give to save herself?

Not the panthers. She couldn't let him sacrifice the mother and the cubs like that. There had to be another way.

# –15–

## The Shadow That Hunts

Kiri's thoughts blurred and melted into each other as she lay against the tree, waiting for her da to return. One second she was thinking of fishing with Paulo. Another, she was picturing the panther in the cage. Then she heard her mother singing. Then her da was telling her stories about the once-were creatures while the cubs played with her. Everything began to crash and swirl together like waves in a bad storm.

Kiri's head spun when she closed her eyes, so she tried to keep them open, but she was so exhausted it was hard to stay awake. She needed to focus on something. Reaching over to her father's pack, she pulled out his waller guidebook. It opened to the entry on the panther he'd referenced.

The sun had set and it was getting dark. She could barely see the letters on the page.

"'*Puma concolor,*'" read Kiri, sounding out the name written beneath the picture of the panther. "Is that who you are?"

She looked at the shadow in the cage. The panther lay on her side, panting, her tongue lolling out. Her eyes were half-open, but she didn't move.

Kiri crawled closer, taking the book with her, and sat near the cage. Snowflake sniffed, clearly disapproving, but he didn't leave her side. He curled up in her lap and groomed himself while she struggled to read more of the description.

There were several other names for the panther in the book. Mountain lion. Cougar. Catamount. Florida panther. Ghost cat. Yet none of the names seemed to fit the creature before her. Not entirely.

The description seemed right, though. Six to seven feet long. Tan coat. Black-tipped ears. Yellow-green eyes. Cubs were described as having spotted fur and blue eyes at birth, which also fit.

In the book, the panther was listed as "critically endangered."

Information on how the panther lived and what it ate followed the description, but the words felt flat and irrelevant to Kiri. They didn't explain why the creature in the cage called to her so powerfully, or what it had to do with her mother. And they didn't explain why it had accepted her and let her play with its cubs. Or why its scratch was killing her now.

"Who are you?" whispered Kiri, leaning toward the cage.

Snowflake stirred and climbed onto Kiri's shoulder. The little rat tugged her hair, as if trying to pull her back. He trembled and chittered, then burrowed into her hood.

*Good idea,* thought Kiri. *Keep your distance.*

Even as she thought this, she continued to lean closer to the cage.

The panther mother blinked, watching Kiri through slit eyes. She seemed awake, but barely. Kiri understood. She felt the same way—not awake, but not able to sleep either. Caught in a between place.

The panther took three deep breaths and Kiri matched them, syncing her breathing to the panther's. She pictured herself the way the panther must see her—not just her tousled appearance, but her soap-scented hair and salty, feverish skin.

Reaching through the wires of the cage, she touched the panther's shoulder. The panther didn't move. Her fur felt surprisingly soft. Kiri sensed the muscle underneath, radiating heat and power. It sent a shiver through her. She imagined feeling a hand on her own shoulder as she stroked the panther's fur—the warm hand of her mother, comforting her. Giving her strength.

The panther closed her eyes, appearing to relax and give in to the tranquilizers. As she did, Kiri closed her eyes too. The warm touch of her mother's hand stayed on her shoulder.

🐢

"Wake up, Cricket!" called her mother. "You need to wake up!"

Kiri stirred, but she didn't see her ma anywhere. She must have been imagining her. *What did it mean when ghosts called you?* she thought.

The sky looked dark and the constellations seemed strange, as if the seasons had changed while she'd been asleep. The land around her appeared horribly empty. No trees. No life. Nothing familiar. Thunder rumbled, signaling the approach of a storm, and stars began to streak across the sky. They spun faster and faster, becoming swirling lines of light until the sky melted into a bright white funnel cloud that clawed at her.

She opened her mouth to scream, and woke again.

The sky was still dark, but the stars looked familiar now. It was late. Several hours had passed since she'd fallen asleep. Where was her da? He should have returned by now.

Kiri felt a rough tongue on her cheek, followed by an urgent nudge. Snowflake pushed his nose against her jaw, trying to wake her.

"It's okay, Snowflake," she muttered, but he didn't stop nudging her. *Get up!* he seemed to say. *You have to get up!*

The thunder she'd heard in her nightmare rumbled again, louder this time.

She turned her head to the side and saw two green eyes shining in the moonlight beside her. The panther was standing and growling.

A jolt of fear surged through Kiri. She scrambled back, scooping Snowflake into her arms. He trembled and tried to burrow into her armpit. All her senses focused on the panther crouched in the cage, inches from where she'd been lying.

The panther's fiery green eyes glinted in the moonlight, and her ears lay flat against her head in a threatening posture. The tranquilizers in the meat must have worn off. With every breath the panther seemed to become more awake, and she was angry.

"Shhh . . . ," said Kiri. "I'm your friend, remember?" She reached a hand out toward the cage, hoping to calm the panther.

The shadow within snarled and lunged, slamming into the walls of the cage.

Kiri jerked her hand back. Her heart pounded, pushing fear through her veins.

The panther growled again, all coiled muscle and bristling wildness seeking release. Kiri's neck prickled. Each growl reverberated deep in her chest, rattling her bones with the uncontainable rage of a mother separated from her cubs.

Fear lashed through Kiri, strong as a hurricane ripping her thoughts away. The devi marks on her shoulder and cheek burned, and her pulse raced. Still, she refused to back away from the growling panther. Then a curious thing happened. Her fear broke apart and she discovered a deeper calm beyond fear.

Sometimes, in the middle of a storm, the sky would clear and the wind would quiet for a short while before it picked up again. Her da called it the eye of the hurricane. Kiri felt as if she were in that eye now. Her breathing deepened. Her pulse slowed. And when she looked at the panther, she finally saw it clearly. It wasn't just one creature, but many. It was all the panthers that had come before it, and all that might come after.

*Puma concolor.* Catamount. Ghost cat. Mountain lion. Florida panther. The Shadow That Hunts. The creature she saw was all of these and more. It was the spirit of wildness itself. And if it stayed in this cage, that spirit would be torn out, and the forest would unravel.

In that moment, Kiri understood several things at once. She knew her da should have returned hours ago. Something had gone wrong—he might have been caught by the fugees, or injured. Eventually the fugees would come looking for her, and when they did, they'd find the panther and kill it. She couldn't let that happen.

Time was running out, both for the panther and for her. But there was one very important thing she could still do. Even though the panther might kill her, she could release it.

Snowflake gave up trying to hide in Kiri's armpit. He clambered onto her shoulder and gave several warning chuffs. She was touched by his attempts to protect her. Despite his small size, he was brave and loyal—a true friend, and that was why he couldn't stay with her.

"Easy, little one," she told Snowflake as she lifted him from her shoulder.

The rat quivered in her hands.

Kiri stroked his head to comfort him while she walked to a nearby palmetto tree. "I'm sorry, Snowflake. I love you, but you need to go now so you don't get hurt."

Snowflake nudged her fingers. *Don't be silly. I'm not leaving you,* he seemed to say.

Kiri kissed the white star on his head and brushed her cheek against his soft pink ears. "You'll be okay," she said, struggling to keep her voice steady. Crying would only make Snowflake more anxious.

She set the rat on a tuft of palm fronds near the top of the palmetto. "Go on, find some other rats. Some nice ones," she said. "That's where you belong."

Snowflake cocked his head. Kiri pulled a palm nut from her hood and gave it to him.

He took the nut in his tiny paws, but immediately dropped it and nudged her fingers again.

"You'll always be my Snowflake. Now go. I have to do this."

She stepped away from Snowflake before she lost courage. The rat squeaked—a high-pitched, desperate squeak, unlike any sound she'd ever heard him make before, but Kiri didn't look back. She couldn't. If she did, she'd fall apart, and she needed all her courage to do what came next.

The panther's growls grew louder as Kiri approached the cage. She reached for the knife on her belt and held it out before her. The blade seemed such a small, insignificant thing. The panther had five blades just as sharp on each of her paws, and jaws strong enough to snap Kiri's bones like twigs. She had eyes that could see in the dark, and ears that could pinpoint mice moving through the grass a dozen steps away. She was many times stronger and faster than Kiri, and she could move in complete silence without being seen.

Kiri had no illusions about the panther anymore. She was a wild predator, and she'd tear through Kiri just as she'd tear through the walls of the cage if she could to get to her cubs. Still, Kiri approached.

Taking a deep breath, Kiri slid the tip of her knife into the gap between the latch and the door. The panther's growls made her stomach quake. Once she did this, there'd be no turning back. She knew that. But she also knew she couldn't live with not doing this. Using all her strength, Kiri pried the knife against the metal bars until the latch snapped and the cage door fell open.

The panther huddled in the shadows at the back of the cage. Kiri closed her eyes, expecting death to come quickly now—a hot bite on her neck or a crushing paw swipe to her head. At least it would be better than withering from fever and dying slowly.

For a moment, all was quiet. The door stayed open, yet nothing happened.

Swift as the wind, the panther leapt.

※

Everything, even the blood flowing through Kiri's veins, stopped.

But the hot bite didn't come. There was no crushing paw strike. No pain. Perhaps death happened faster than she imagined.

She opened her eyes, expecting to see whatever the dead saw. The trees, grass, and ruins all looked the same as before. The cage door gaped open in front of her, but the cage appeared empty. The prowling shadow within had vanished.

Kiri scanned the forest, spotting the panther less than a stone's throw from where she crouched. Moonlight glinted off the panther's fiery green eyes as the creature studied her.

*Follow,* whispered a voice that sounded less like her mother, and more like the hiss of a cat.

# PART III

*Devi of the Sky*

# –16–

## The Tree in the Desert

*Follow.*

That's what the voice said, so that's what Kiri did. She walked after the Shadow That Hunts, as if the death she'd faced when she unlocked the cage had merely been a test she had to pass.

She couldn't tell when or how it had happened, but the whole world was a shimmering desert. Her skin burned and hot sand singed her bare feet. Kiri stumbled as she climbed the dunes. The withered limbs of trees jutted above the sand in places like half-buried giants, their wooden fingers crumbling the moment she touched them. She saw no tracks. No birds or insects. No telltale green of living plants. Just a shifting, empty expanse of sand and the pale blue of a cloudless sky.

Wind pushed the dunes, moving them like tired waves in a blazing ocean. Walls and fences crisscrossed the landscape, but they couldn't hold back the sand. Even the buildings in the distance appeared empty and barren—hollowed out by the unstoppable wind and the blowing sand.

Kiri wondered if it was the wind that had caused everything to die. Or was it the heat that had turned all the plants to dust? Either way, the emptiness had come, leaving only hot sand beneath her feet and a shadow walking ahead of her.

The shadow drifted so far ahead that it became a speck in the distance. Then the speck stretched into a tree.

Kiri stumbled toward it. Where there was a tree, there had to be shade. And water.

The tree looked enormous—a sprawling banyan with a trunk several times wider than Kiri could spread her arms, and branches that dropped roots deep into the dunes around it. But it had almost no leaves. Nearly every branch was bare.

Kiri's hopes withered when she saw this, until she noticed a woman near the base. The woman had chestnut skin and thin black braids tied back into a cluster that sprouted like a fountain of hair from the top of her head.

"Ma?" Kiri whispered as she approached.

Her mother didn't look up. She knelt and dipped one finger into a bucket, then placed drops of water one by one on tiny blades of dune grass poking through the sand.

"What are you doing?" asked Kiri.

"Without the grass the sand will blow and tear the leaves from the tree," replied her mother. "Without the leaves the tree will die. Without the tree the birds will starve. Without the birds the sky will weep. Without the sky the fish can't breathe. Without the fish the people will starve." She sat back on her heels and stared at Kiri. "Nothing stands alone."

"I've been looking for you," said Kiri, rushing toward her mother.

But her mother didn't smile or pull her into a hug as Kiri expected. "I can't call you here anymore," she said. "It's too dangerous. You must become what you seek."

Kiri frowned, confused.

"Tend the tree," said her mother. She gestured to three green leaves on a nearby branch. They were some of the only leaves left on the banyan. "If it dies all will unravel, and there's no wall that can stop the unraveling." As she spoke, she walked around the wide tree trunk. "Tend the tree," she repeated.

Kiri hurried after her, but when she reached the other side of the tree she didn't see her mother. "Ma? Where are you?"

*Kiri, Kiri, Cricket . . . ,* replied a whisper that was above her, and behind her, and close to her, and not there at all.

"Ma!" cried Kiri.

*Hear the crickets chirping in the grass,* sang her mother in a voice so distant and faint, Kiri couldn't tell which direction it came from.

*If they're alone, they'll be the last.*
*When the wind blows, a storm will come*
*Little crickets must run, run, run!*

*"Kir!"*

Kiri startled awake, heart racing from her vision.

Her head spun and she felt terribly hot and thirsty. She blinked several times, trying to steady her sight. As her eyes adjusted she saw a black shadow above her, only it wasn't a tree. It wasn't her mother, either.

It was a crow, perched on the edge of a ruin wall. The crow opened its black beak and cawed again. *"Kir! Kir!"* It cocked its head, peering down at her with one yellow-rimmed eye, then the other.

Kiri sat up, recognizing the jagged walls of the ruin. She wasn't very far from the clearing with the panther's den.

Gradually, images from the night fell into place. She must have passed out in the ruins after following the panther, and then she'd dreamed of the tree. Only it didn't seem like an ordinary dream. Her fever visions felt as real as anything else.

"Kiri!" called a distant voice.

The crow squawked *"Kir!"* again, as if imitating the call. With a flap of wings it launched itself into the sky and circled above her. The devi marks on Kiri's shoulder and cheek tingled as she watched it.

"Kiri!" called the voice again. A man's voice—one of the fugees from the village. Kiri couldn't tell who.

Every muscle in her body ached when she forced herself to climb down from the ruin and go toward where the person calling her name seemed to be. After a few minutes, she saw a couple of figures moving through the forest in the distance. She slowed and crouched behind a clump of muhly grass. Nessa and Tarun appeared to be searching the ground, along with a few other fugees. Kiri made out Tae's skinny form in the early-morning light. Then she saw Senek and Charro step out from between two clusters of saw palms beyond them. Tarun put his hands to his mouth and shouted her name again.

Kiri almost ran to them. They carried food and water. They could give her a drink and take care of her. Her mouth gaped at the prospect of gulping down cool water. Then she saw the long gun Charro cradled in his arms. She couldn't trust them. Not if her da wasn't there.

Kiri crept closer, careful to stay hidden behind bushes and stands of muhly grass.

"Anything?" asked Tarun.

Charro shook his head.

"The tracks led this way," said Nessa. "She must be around here somewhere."

"Which tracks?" asked Charro.

"Both hers and the panther's," said Tarun, gesturing to the ground. "At least until here. Then the trails split."

"Where's the Waller Man?" asked Nessa, scanning the area near where Kiri hid.

Kiri froze, not even daring to breathe, but the fugees didn't see her.

"He's with Paulo," said Charro. "They're searching along the fence line east of here."

Kiri's heart sped up at the mention of her da. He was out searching for her with the fugees! When he'd discovered the panther and her missing, he must have persuaded the fugees to help him find her. There was still hope. Kiri almost called to the fugees, but something held her back. Her mother's voice echoed in her head. *Run, run, run!* she'd said, warning her to get away.

"We should tell him about the tracks," said Nessa.

"Tell him what?" countered Charro. "We haven't found the girl."

"Or the panther," added Senek.

Charro gave Senek a sharp look, then he turned back to address Tarun and Nessa. "We don't know if she was following the panther, or if the panther was hunting her. All we know is that their tracks are together and then they're not. You going to tell her da that she might have been eaten?"

"I didn't see any blood," said Nessa.

"Not yet," answered Charro.

Crouched behind the bush, Kiri stayed silent. Did they think the panther had attacked her? Was that why they were searching for her? Or did Charro have other motives?

"He's right," said Tarun. "We shouldn't get her da until we know more. No sense scaring him like that."

"You and Nessa head east toward the fence line," said

Charro. "If you find her trail, give a shout. And if you don't, go north."

"What are you going to do?" asked Nessa.

"Senek, Tae, and I will search inland, toward the lake. She must have crossed this way somewhere. We just have to find her trail again."

Nessa clenched her jaw, but she seemed to accept the plan. "Why on earth did she release that thing?" she asked, shaking her head.

"Who knows?" said Charro. "If you find her, you can ask her."

"*When*," said Nessa. "*When* we find her."

Charro nodded. "When," he said, and the group split up.

Nessa and Tarun passed through the tall grass only a few steps from where Kiri hid. They were so focused on searching the ground for tracks that they didn't notice her, and she didn't make a sound.

Tae and Senek started to head in the opposite direction, toward the lake, but Charro paused near a ridge of sand oaks and cabbage palms. He snapped his fingers, signaling for Tae and Senek to wait.

"What is it? You see something?" asked Tae.

Charro put a finger to his lips.

Kiri crawled closer so she could hear what he said. Charro waited until Nessa and Tarun were out of earshot before he spoke again.

"We're not going that way," said Charro.

"But you said west, toward the lake," replied Tae.

Charro cocked the long gun and checked the sights. "We're going this way instead."

"Why?" asked Tae.

"Because I saw some tracks over there."

"Kiri's tracks?"

"No. Panther tracks," said Charro, keeping his voice low. "Fresh ones. We're close."

He set off, heading straight toward the clearing with the den, long gun raised and ready.

Kiri's chest clenched so tightly she could barely breathe. Charro and the others weren't trying to help her da find her. They were looking for the panther, and she'd led them right to the panther's trail.

She couldn't let anyone find the den, especially not Charro. If Charro found it, he'd catch the cubs and trade them to the boat people. Then the cubs would be separated and sold on the black market, or killed and skinned. Cricket, Skitter, and Mustache would be lost, all because of her.

"Stay alert," Charro said, glancing back at Tae and Senek. "It's time we take what's ours."

# –17–

# The Space Between the Living and the Dead

As soon as Charro, Senek, and Tae were gone, Kiri set off through the ghost forest, swift as the Shadow That Hunts. At least, that's how she tried to run, jumping over logs and landing lightly on her toes, bounding like the panther did. But her body was weaker than she had thought, and she tripped and almost smacked into a tree.

Kiri picked herself up off the sandy ground and continued on as fast as she could. Hours ago she'd been dizzy and exhausted, but now she passed into a realm beyond exhaustion. Every muscle in her body felt as if it were on fire. In her fever-struck mind, she pictured layer after layer of the self she knew burning off until there was nothing but a glowing coal at her core that refused to be extinguished.

She had to hurry. Charro, Senek, and Tae would follow

the tracks right to the den, but they didn't know the area as well as she did. By circling around and taking a gully through the forest, Kiri hoped to get ahead of them. Then she could work backward, starting near the den and erasing all the tracks that led to it so Charro wouldn't find the cubs.

The first slivers of sunlight crested the horizon when she approached the clearing, painting the clouds red. Red sky in the morning meant storms would come—that's what the netters said. In the rosy light Kiri could make out the thick saw palm bushes where the den was hidden, but she didn't see the cubs anywhere.

*Good,* she thought. Hopefully, they were all safe in the den with their mother. Kiri spotted several round divots in the sandy earth—fresh panther tracks, large and small, dotting the area. The tracks were thickest around the opening of the den.

*Stay in there,* she thought, staring at the dark mouth of the den. *Don't come out. Don't let yourself be seen.* She concentrated on the words, willing the cubs to understand. If they came out and were spotted by the fugees, she wouldn't be able to save them.

With a couple of dry palm branches Kiri brushed away any tracks she could find. She didn't go too close to the den, focusing instead on tracks that might lead Charro there. As she worked, images of the cubs and their playful antics flickered through her head. *Stay safe, safe, safe,* she chanted to herself, picturing each of the cubs. Whether it was because of the warnings or the noise she made, the cubs didn't come out.

Kiri left the clearing and followed the most recent line of tracks back toward where she'd last seen Charro and the others, dragging the palm branches behind her. It was a trick her da had taught her. The stiff palm leaves would wipe out tracks, both hers and the panthers', in the sandy earth. Her heart pounded as she glanced back repeatedly to check her progress. One missed print and Charro might find the whole family.

Sweat poured down Kiri's sides, and her hands stung from dragging the palm branches, but she didn't stop. *Tend the tree*, her mother had told her. Even though Kiri didn't know exactly what that meant, it seemed connected to the cubs. There'd been three leaves on the tree in her vision— one leaf for each cub. The more she worked, the more the devi mark on her shoulder warmed, as if her mother's hand were resting there, encouraging her. So she pressed on, erasing the panther tracks, doing everything she could to save them.

After some time, Kiri sensed that she wasn't alone. A shadow moved through the grass at the edge of her vision. At first her fever-struck mind let her believe it was her mother, walking with her. She turned to focus on her, but the shadow vanished in the brush, causing a few low leaves to stir. *No,* she thought, realizing it wasn't her mother.

"Go away," she whispered to the shadows behind her. "It's dangerous here."

Nothing moved in the grass and brush behind her. She continued on, erasing any tracks she found until she sensed the shadow again.

This time, Kiri resisted turning around. Her da had told her once that eyes were more sensitive to light around the edges, so if you wanted to see dim stars, the trick was to avoid looking directly at them. She tried to do that now, slowly turning her head while focusing on the shadows at the edge of her vision. When nothing moved for several moments, she realized with a start that she was staring right at her observer: in the brush off to the side crouched the panther mother, perfectly camouflaged among the dry undergrowth.

"I'm trying to save you, but you have to help me," Kiri whispered. Her throat tightened as she considered how close Charro must be by now. "Go back to your den."

The panther didn't move, and Kiri began to feel desperate. "Please. Go away."

The panther's fiery green eyes burned into Kiri for a moment longer. Then the panther focused her senses on something to the side. All was quiet.

A shot rang out, shattering the morning stillness.

"Run!" shouted Kiri.

The panther was already moving. It bolted from the grass not ten feet from where Kiri stood.

Kiri's heart pounded. "Go, go, go!"

The panther bounded away, swift as water slipping through grasping fingers. It was all right—the shot must have missed. Nothing could catch the panther now. She was too fast and powerful.

Kiri beamed as she watched the panther dart through the ghost forest, muscles bunching and reaching. She leapt over logs with unspeakable grace. Kiri had never seen anything so beautiful.

But when the panther reached the clearing, her steps weren't so quick and graceful anymore. She stumbled, dragging her muzzle across the ground. Then she raised her head and continued on in an odd skipping gait, one of her front paws raised.

Kiri gasped—it couldn't be.

She sprinted after the panther, a cry lodged in her throat.

By the time Kiri entered the clearing, the panther mother was almost halfway across. Halfway to the den. She stumbled in the tall grass and didn't reappear.

Kiri raced through the tall grass, not caring how the leaves scratched and cut her. Her stomach dropped when she saw the panther lying on her side. She staggered closer, not believing her eyes.

The panther's tawny fur, matted with blood, glistened in the early-morning light. For a few seconds the panther's legs continued to move, reaching for earth that was no longer beneath her paws. Then they stopped.

"No," whispered Kiri. She knelt by the panther, half

expecting the creature to growl and lunge at her like she'd done before. She'd welcome the panther's snarls and fierceness now, but the panther barely moved. Her breath came in and out in a ragged way. So did Kiri's. "You can't die," she whispered. "I can't lose you."

"Stay back! Don't go near it!" shouted a gruff voice.

Charro barreled across the clearing toward her, long gun clutched in his hands, but Kiri ignored him.

She reached out to touch the soft fur of the panther's neck. A shiver coursed through her. She didn't remember losing her mother. She couldn't recall a single thing about the day her ma had died. But Kiri knew she'd always remember this. The warm softness of the panther's fur. The sticky smell of blood. The sound of the panther's last breaths. The red glow of the rising sun. It wasn't just the panther that she was losing. She felt as if her connection to her ma, and the wild wonder that made such connections possible, was being torn away. *This can't happen!* she wanted to scream.

The panther's fiery green eyes remained open, only they weren't focused on Kiri. Instead, the panther's gaze seemed fixed on something in the distance. Kiri knew exactly what the panther was looking for and where she'd been running to. The realization hollowed out a place in Kiri's chest. The cubs would be like her now. Motherless. Lost.

"I'll take care of them," whispered Kiri. "I'll keep them safe. I promise."

Perhaps the panther understood, because she seemed

to relax. Her breath shuddered out once more, but not in. Then there was no breath at all.

"Get back!" shouted Charro.

Kiri buried her face in the panther's side, willing the creature to breathe again. It made no difference. The panther remained horribly still. There was only the lingering warmth of her body, and soon the warmth, too, would be gone.

"Crazy waller girl," said Charro, pulling Kiri away from the panther's body. "You almost got yourself killed."

# —18—

## Kiri's Promise

All three search parties rushed to the clearing, called by the sound of the gunshot. Kiri heard Nessa, Tarun, and Paulo arrive. Not long after, her da was by her side and hugging her, but she barely felt it.

The adults began arguing. Charro claimed salvage rights to the panther's body, to which her da responded with the same sort of angry disbelief as when the sea turtle had been killed. "Salvage rights? That's why you shot it? For salvage rights?"

His accusations provoked Charro into his own blustery outrage. "I saved your daughter, Waller Man. The panther was hunting her. Senek saw. It was in the grass, stalking her. If I hadn't shot it, she'd be dead."

"I needed it alive."

"Would you prefer I let the panther eat her?"

"You could have scared it off. Done something else."

This time, Kiri didn't try to stop the argument. What was the point? She kept running her fingers through the panther's tawny fur, watching the dust whirl into the air. How could something so beautiful be dead? How could a devi be dead?

"Greedy wallers," snapped Charro. "All you care about are the things you can get. I saved her. You should be thanking me."

"I needed the panther alive to get Kiri medicine," said Martin.

Charro was silent for a moment. "It's still worth something," he replied. "The boat people will trade plenty for it. Tell you what—I'll split my salvage with you. Maybe the boat people will have the medicine she needs."

Her da cursed and paced by the panther's body. Kiri wanted to shoo him away so she could be alone with her sadness. Couldn't they see what she'd lost? What they'd all lost? How could they keep arguing?

"I've already contacted my patrons," continued her da. "They're sending a cargo tridrone at first light. When they find out the panther's been shot . . . You're not going to get anything for this, Charro. None of us are. You didn't save my daughter. You robbed her of her best chance."

At this, Kiri looked up. Was her da saying that she was going to die now too? She knew she was sick. She hadn't forgotten her fever. But she'd thought now that her da was here, he'd find a way to save her. Was he saying he couldn't?

"Wait," said Paulo. "Look."

Kiri glanced at her friend, but he didn't look back at her. He seemed to be staring at something else across the clearing. "Think the wallers will trade medicine for that?" he asked, pointing at the saw palms.

One of the cubs peeked out between two palm leaves at the mouth of the den. Kiri recognized his startling blue eyes and fluffy white paws.

*Cricket.*

Her first thought was to chase him back into the den, only it was too late. The curious spotted cub was always the first out of the den, and the first to bound toward his mother when she returned. Brave, adventurous Cricket had already given himself away.

Cricket stalked out of the den, growling and with hackles raised. Did he smell his mother's presence? Was he coming to protect her?

"By the devi," said Charro, seeing the cub.

Martin gasped and stepped closer to the den.

The cub's siblings, Mustache and Skitter, lingered in the mouth of the den behind him. Their spotted fur had kept them camouflaged in the dappled shade of the palm leaves, yet the more they moved, the more visible they became.

*No,* thought Kiri. *Stay hidden!* Her head reeled and her vision blurred. She didn't want others to see the cubs, and she didn't want the cubs to see their dead mother. Everything was going wrong at once.

"Three of them," said Martin, continuing to edge toward the den.

"Not so fast, Waller," grumbled Charro. He cocked the long gun. "You don't get to take all of them. These belong to the village. We need the food and supplies that trading them will provide."

"Be reasonable, Charro," said Martin. He'd unslung the fancy waller gun from his shoulder. "These need to go to the wallers."

Anger swelled up and broke loose in Kiri as she realized what Charro and her da were discussing. "Stop!" she yelled.

She stumbled toward the den, putting herself between the humans and the cubs she'd promised to protect. "You can't have them."

Both her da and Charro froze. Each of them held a gun, and they seemed torn between aiming at each other and aiming at the cubs.

"They're not yours. I won't let you take them." Kiri tried to sound fierce, but her voice faltered. A buzzing filled her ears, like a thousand angry flies approaching.

She thought the sound was only in her head. Then it grew louder and everyone looked up.

"You can't take them!" she shouted to the sky, and the flies, and the cruel day that had already taken far too much.

A tridrone descended over the clearing, drowning out her protests.

The tridrone was the same dragonfly shape as the one that had landed on the beach several days before, only several times bigger. Two people could be seen through the dark, bulbous windows of the head, and the abdomen looked big enough to swallow a stilt house. One of the figures waved at Martin, whose satphone blinked with an urgent red light.

"*Drop your weapons!*" ordered the pilot from speakers on the tridrone's belly.

Martin set down his rifle and shouted for Charro to do the same, but Charro didn't listen. He hunched over his gun and bolted into the cover of the pines surrounding the clearing.

Kiri didn't see what the adults did next. She was too concerned with herding the cubs back into the den before the waller pilot spotted them. If the wallers didn't see the cubs, they might let them be. Then she could take care of them and keep them safe, like she'd promised their mother.

"Go!" Kiri shouted to the cubs. "Get away from here!"

Cricket flattened his black-tipped ears and refused to move. His gaze remained fixed on his mother's body in the grass.

Kiri waved her hands menacingly at the cub, not caring if he scratched or bit her as long as she got him to go back under the cover of the saw palm bushes.

"*Drop your weapons and lie down on the ground,*" ordered the pilot. "*This is your final warning.*"

Instead of running away, Cricket prowled forward and sniffed Kiri's hand. He must have smelled his mother's scent on her, because he immediately stopped bristling and brushed his head against her fingers. His eyes were the same stunning blue that the sea turtle's had been.

Kiri pulled her hand back. "No. Get away from me," she said. "Your mother is dead, understand? Because of me she's dead! You have to hide!"

The cub didn't leave. He swiped at her leg like she was playing a game.

"*On the ground now or you will be shot!*" boomed the pilot.

Kiri heard her da calling to her, but she ignored him. She had to scare Cricket back into the bushes. She reached for her mother's knife, thinking that the shiny blade might startle him enough to send him running into the den.

The shot hit her shoulder and knocked her off her feet. She skidded across the ground, clenching her eyes against the pain. Then she felt a rough tongue licking her cheek.

Cricket was still there, protecting her now.

*Go home,* she tried to tell him, but her mouth would barely move. Pain spread from her shoulder to her chest to her heart, dragging her into darkness.

# —19—

## Reflection Between Lives

Kiri had never talked with anyone about how she pictured death. It wasn't something fugees in the village liked to talk about. And it wasn't something she felt she could discuss with her da.

For fugees, death was an ocean engulfing an island— something surrounding them that had to be constantly struggled against, otherwise it would wash away the land. Kiri knew most fugees believed in ghosts. It wasn't uncommon to see a netter standing with his back to the forest and his hands clasped over his ears because a ghost was calling to him and he didn't want to listen to it. Or to see a woman walking briskly away from the waste pits, telling some spirit behind her to go bug someone else.

The ghosts that fugees claimed to see usually weren't

scary. The opposite, actually. Fugees talked about ghosts as if they were friendly, enticing figures, and *that* was why they wouldn't speak to them. They believed that if they paid attention to ghosts, they'd be lured away from life, and death would claim them as sure as the ocean claiming an insect that landed too close to the waves.

There was only one day of the year when it was acceptable for fugees to speak to the dead. On the fall solstice, when night first became longer than day, each family made a feast for the ones they'd lost. They set out blankets near the edge of the forest and sat and talked with spirits for hours, pouring cups of palm wine for guests no one else could see. They even brought flowers and toys and other objects for the ghosts to enjoy.

Sometimes Kiri saw women crying and laughing with the children they'd lost. Or men nodding as they listened to the voices of fathers who'd died. But when the sun set, they buried all the food, flowers, and toys, and folded up their blankets. They walked back to the fires burning in the village and didn't speak of the dead again for another year, no matter how many times the dead tried to speak to them.

For the fugees, death wasn't a mystery or another world. It was as common as hunger. Everyone in the village had lost someone. Death was the norm and life the exception, and so death had to be struggled against for life to persist.

For wallers, death was something else entirely—at least, that was the sense of it Kiri had gotten from her da. He never talked about death or what he thought happened after someone died, but he'd made it clear that he thought the fugee feasts for the dead were a ridiculous waste of time and resources, and their claims of seeing ghosts were superstitious nonsense. Death, as he saw it, was simply the absence of life—a void that was pointless to contemplate, and discussing what happened after death would be like discussing why two plus two didn't equal five. It simply didn't, and that was that.

As far back as Kiri could remember, though, she'd imagined death differently. She didn't see it as something to be struggled against in a constant tug-of-war between the living and the dead. And it wasn't an absence to be ignored, either. Instead, she'd always pictured death as this: a mirror.

But not an ordinary mirror.

Death, as Kiri imagined it, was a mirror that reflected all of life. In death, everything she'd experienced—all the people she'd known and all the things she'd seen, touched, tasted, smelled, and heard—could be reflected back to her. She could experience any moment over and over again until she finally understood it. And when she was ready, she might tumble back into life to collect new experiences and find a new death.

Kiri sometimes wondered if there might be other worlds besides this one that she could live in, or maybe she'd be reborn as other creatures in this world. But between each life there'd be a place of reflection, like a room full of mirrors bouncing light back and forth until it blurred into one experience, and she became the mirror. Because life needed to see itself reflected somewhere.

So Kiri didn't fear death, and she didn't think death would be paradise, either. She thought it could be both a beautiful and a terrible place, depending on what experiences she collected and how she reflected those experiences back to herself. That's why she wasn't surprised to find herself, after being shot and losing consciousness, in a room where the air felt cool and crisp, as it did on the mornings by the shore that she'd always liked best. Nor was she surprised to find herself bathed in warm light, with the softest ground beneath her.

What was a surprise, though, was the sky. The clouds were dark blue instead of white, and the air between them glowed as orange as the center of a honeysuckle flower. While Kiri studied the clouds, three enormous purple birds flew past, with long, forked tails that streamed behind them like ribbons in a breeze. A strange fake-flowery smell tinged the air as well.

Nothing she saw or smelled seemed close to anything she'd experienced in life before. The sky, clouds, and long-tailed purple birds were entirely new to her.

As she considered how this could be, it dawned on her that she might not have died after all.

# –20–

# Walls and Sleep

"Oh, you're awake," said a woman leaning over Kiri. She wore a crisp white shirt and had straight, shiny hair. She didn't look up at the orange sky with blue clouds, not even when a flock of green-feathered snakes with yellow stripes fluttered past. "How is your comfort level?"

Kiri lifted a finger to point at the sky.

The woman finally glanced up, right as what appeared to be a gigantic red alligator with four black wings flew a loop. She shook her head and made a *tsk-tsk* sound. "The night nurse must have done that," she said, speaking in a terse way that sounded odd to Kiri. Then the woman reached out and touched something on a nearby vid screen.

A moment later, the sky changed. Now it was light blue

with white clouds. It looked almost normal, except that several kittens played on the clouds, chasing balls of string.

"There. Better?" asked the woman.

"It's a vid!" said Kiri. "The sky is all a vid!" She stared in wonder, having never seen a vid screen so big or realistic before.

The woman sighed and shook her head. "You're a very lucky girl, you know. In all my years as a nurse, this is the first time I've ever seen someone as old as you get a bio-visa."

"Bio-visa?" asked Kiri.

The woman pointed to a cluster of thin black, green, and purple lines on the inside of Kiri's wrist. It looked similar to her da's waller mark, except it was smaller and shaped like a blackbird feather, with the odd rainbow sheen of oil on water. Kiri tried rubbing the mark, but it seemed etched into her skin.

"Careful. The nano ink is still setting. It had to be installed before you could be given treatment. You must have some very influential friends to be granted a mark like that."

*Friends?* thought Kiri. She looked up at the woman, wondering what friends she could be talking about, but her gaze kept sliding past the woman to the kittens frolicking on the clouds. They looked almost like the panther cubs. And with that thought, Kiri's jaw clenched and stomach twisted. The cubs were in danger. They needed her. "Where are the cubs?" she asked, trying to sit up.

The woman made the *tsk-tsk* sound again and pushed

her back down, which wasn't hard. Kiri felt so dizzy and weak she could barely lift her head. Still, she had to find the cubs.

"Well, aren't you a feisty one?" said the woman. She pushed a button on a box with a tube attached to it that led to Kiri's arm. "I suppose you need to be, to survive out there."

"Please, where are the cubs?" repeated Kiri.

"Cubs?" The woman gave her a perplexed look, as if she'd asked about once-were creatures.

Kiri realized the woman had no idea what she was talking about. She kept struggling to get up, but a warm heaviness spread from her arm through her chest, taking her strength away.

Finally, Kiri lay back and tried to assess where she was. The glow of the sky illuminated the plain white walls of a room. She was lying on a strange raised bed, with metal railings on each side of her and several wires and tubes going from her arms to machines next to the bed.

"There. That's better," said the woman. "Now, how is your comfort level?"

Kiri frowned at the woman. Why did she keep asking about her comfort?

"Do. You. Com-pre-hend. What. I. Am. Say-ing?" asked the woman, separating each syllable like they were wooden blocks stacked together.

" 'Com-pre-hend'?" echoed Kiri, imitating the way the woman spoke.

"Is that a yes, or are you mocking me?"

The woman reminded Kiri of an angry squirrel, chittering down at her from a branch. "You sound strange."

"In what way?"

"Your words are all square corners." Kiri decided that this was better than calling the woman an angry squirrel.

At this, Squirrel Woman rolled her eyes and turned her attention to the vid screen next to Kiri's bed. "Well, we can't all have your quaint cadences, now, can we?" she said. "Or the colorful vocabulary coastal refugees use. What is it they call it? Pigeon gumbo?"

Kiri realized this must have been a question, but she had no idea why Squirrel Woman was asking her about pigeons. And what were kittens doing chasing balls of string on clouds?

"Your comfort level," repeated Squirrel Woman. She seemed in a hurry to be elsewhere.

Kiri thought of the cubs again and fought to get up, but her body was so heavy and weak. She moved her arm and noticed that the tube taped to her ended in a needle that went under her skin. They were drugging her! That was why she felt weak. She reached to pull the tube out.

"No, no!" snapped Squirrel Woman. She pushed Kiri's arm back down and reached to press the button on the tube box again.

"What is it?" asked Kiri. "What are you doing to me?"

Before the nurse could respond, her da burst into the room.

Martin took one look at Kiri, then scowled at Squirrel Woman. "Why didn't you tell us she was awake? You were given strict instructions."

"And I followed them to the letter," replied the nurse, releasing Kiri's arm. "She only regained consciousness a moment ago."

Martin hurried to Kiri's side. "Are you okay, Kiribati? I wanted to be here when you woke."

"There are tubes in my arms." Kiri raised her arms to show her da all the wires and tubes attached to them.

Squirrel Woman frowned, but she didn't push Kiri's arms down again.

"It's only temporary," said her da. "It's how they're giving you medicine for the infection. They treated you just in time."

"The doctor says you're going to make a full recovery," chimed in another woman, who'd followed Martin into the room. Unlike the nurse, this woman wore darker, softer-looking clothing. She had dark skin as well—darker than Kiri's, even, which surprised Kiri. She'd thought all wallers had pale skin that turned red in the sun, like her da's.

"This is Dr. Sonia," said Martin, introducing the waller woman. "She's vice president of acquisitions at Gen Tech, one of my patrons. It's because of Sonia's influence that we were able to get you treated."

"Your father is our top field collector," said Sonia, standing close to Martin. "His work's been so exceptional that we decided to make a few exceptions for him." She smiled and brushed Kiri's unruly hair back from her face.

Compared with the nurse's touch, Sonia's fingers on her cheek felt surprisingly gentle.

"How's your shoulder feel?" asked her da.

Kiri moved the shoulder that the panther had scratched. The wound was still there, but it didn't feel hot and itchy anymore.

"Not that one," said her da. "The other one."

Kiri winced as she moved her other shoulder. She wondered why it hurt, until she remembered trying to scare the cubs back into the den and being hit in the shoulder by something sharp that threw her to the ground.

"I was shot," said Kiri.

"Yes. We're terribly sorry about that," said Sonia, still smoothing Kiri's wild hair back. "Fortunately, they only used rubber bullets with tranquilizer capsules. The shot left quite a bruise on your shoulder, but no permanent damage."

"They were afraid you were going to harm the cubs after what happened to the adult panther," explained her da.

"Are the cubs okay?" asked Kiri.

"They will be."

"Where are they?"

"Here, actually," said Sonia. "In the animal care ward. This is one of Gen Tech's most advanced facilities. They're receiving the best medical care in the city."

Kiri struggled to sit up. "I have to see them."

"Easy . . . ," said her da. "You need rest, Kiribati. You're still healing."

"But I promised I'd take care of them."

"Promised who?" asked her da.

"The panther mother."

Sonia and Martin shared a concerned look.

"I'm all they have," added Kiri, recalling how Cricket had stayed with her and licked her cheek after she'd been shot. "They need me."

"The cubs are fine," said Martin.

*No*, thought Kiri. *They're not fine. None of us are fine.* She pictured the tree in the desert with only three leaves left. *Without the leaves, the tree will die,* her mother had said. Kiri almost told her da about her visions and her mother's warnings, but she knew he'd dismiss them as fever dreams. They felt too real and important to dismiss, though. And Kiri's sense that the cubs needed her was real, too.

"I have to see them," repeated Kiri. "It's important. . . ."

"Shhh . . . ," said her da.

"No! I have to . . ." Kiri kicked and tried to roll out of bed. "Why won't you let me?"

"Keep her still!" snapped the nurse. She pushed the button on the tube box a few more times.

Kiri reached to pull the tube out, but the nurse caught her hand and held her down.

"Rest, Kiribati." Her da stroked her hair. "Everything's going to be okay."

"It's not. . . ." A warm tingle swept through her, starting from her arm and filling her chest. She suddenly felt so heavy she could barely talk. "No wall will stop . . ."

Whatever the box had pumped into her arm made her unable to keep her eyes open or her mouth moving.

"No more disturbances," said the nurse. "Since she cannot be trusted to lie still, she'll need to be sedated until she completes her drip. Doctor's orders."

# –21–

## Escape

The next time she woke beneath the kitten-cloud sky, Kiri didn't feel so heavy, and her vision wasn't so blurry, and she didn't get dizzy when she moved. She checked her arms and was relieved to find no tubes in them. Except for a couple of wire pads taped to her wrists and neck, and the odd feather-shaped waller mark on her arm, she seemed back to normal. One thing that hadn't gone away, though, was her fear that the cubs were in danger.

She swung her legs off the bed and tried to stand, but one of the wires taped to her wrist got caught on the railing and popped off. Immediately, a screen on the wall began to *BEEP! BEEP! BEEP!*

A man dressed in white burst into the room. He strode

to the screen and pressed a few buttons on a keypad. The alarm stopped.

"If you need something, use the caller," said the man, pointing to a rectangular pad attached to the side of Kiri's bed. "You're not supposed to go anywhere without supervision."

"I need to pee," said Kiri.

The man peeled the other wire pads off her neck and wrist. "There you go," he said, nodding to a door near the entrance to her room.

Kiri took the hint and shuffled through the door into the largest bathroom she'd ever seen. The man let her have a moment to herself. When she was done, she turned to wash her hands and was startled by the face that gazed back at her in the mirror.

At first, she thought it must be a vid of her ma. She leaned forward, and when the image in front of her did the same, Kiri realized it was her reflection. Her face seemed longer, more angular, and less childish than she remembered, in part due to the pale scar on her cheek from where the sea turtle bone had cut her. The biggest change, though, was her hair. Instead of a wild, motherless tangle storming about her head with twigs and leaves stuck in it, her hair had been washed, brushed, and wrestled into several thin braids, just like her mother's.

"Everything okay in there?" asked the man through the door.

"I'm fine," said Kiri. She found a hand mirror in the

bathroom drawer and took it back to bed with her. The nurse reattached the sticky wire pads to her wrists and temples. He didn't talk nearly as much as Squirrel Woman had, but Kiri didn't mind. He was gentler than she'd been.

While the nurse worked, Kiri looked again at her reflection in the hand mirror. Her da had never been able to braid hair like this, so who had done it? And how long had she been asleep?

"Need anything else?" asked the man once all the wires were reattached.

Kiri shook her head, watching the small braids slap against her cheeks, soft as summer rain.

The man turned to do something with the screen on the wall behind her bed. Kiri tilted the mirror she held so that she could see his hands. He punched several numbers into the keypad on the wall and pressed a red button on the screen that said ALARM ON.

Then he left.

*

Kiri didn't catch all the numbers, but she recalled the pattern the nurse's finger had made. As soon as the door clicked shut behind him, she turned toward the screen on the wall, careful not to dislodge any of the wires attached to her arms and neck. Then she repeated the pattern the nurse had used on the keypad, going down the column on the right side and up to the top again.

3-6-9-3

The screen beeped twice in response. Kiri pulled off the wires. No alarm sounded this time, and no one ran in to yell at her. So far, so good.

She stood and shuffled to the door. The last thing she remembered, before Squirrel Woman had held her down and drugged her, was her da refusing to take her to see the panther cubs. If he wouldn't take her to them, she'd find them herself.

Her feet tingled and her head felt light, but her strength seemed to be coming back. She cracked open the door and peeked out.

Strange as the kitten-cloud sky had been, that was nothing compared with what Kiri encountered in the hall. First, there was the music. It sounded like women singing underwater. Then there was the floor. Divided into two halves, each moved in a different direction. The most disorienting thing, though, were the walls. They weren't plain white or flat like the ones in her room. Instead, they arched overhead and shimmered with blue light, as if the hall was really a giant glass tube submerged beneath the cleanest, most pure part of the ocean. Dozens of orange fish swam by, just on the other side of the arched wall, along with other, more fantastic things. In the few seconds Kiri stood peering out, she saw ten or twelve people that were half human, half fish swim toward her.

She knew it had to be a vid screen, but it looked so real. Then the sea people gazed down and waved at her.

"Hello, resident," they said together in odd, bubbly voices.

Kiri was so startled she nearly fell back. She didn't understand how images on a screen could see her, but they continued to stare straight at her and wave.

Each sea person had a name written on his or her seaweed swimsuit. She recognized Squirrel Woman and the male nurse who'd just been in her room. At least, their faces looked similar, but their bodies were different—more muscular and trim—and their legs were fish tails. When they didn't stop waving, Kiri raised a wary hand and waved back. That seemed to satisfy the vid images. All at once, they stopped waving and swam off in various directions.

Kiri glanced down the hall, fearing that one of the nurses would put her back in bed, but no one came. Maybe it was only a trick and the vid images hadn't really seen her. Or maybe they didn't care where she went.

Regardless, Kiri needed to get out of there. She had to find the panther cubs, and fast. If she was confused by this place, they must be terrified. She could practically hear them whimpering. Who knew what the wallers were doing to them?

Kiri stepped out onto the moving hallway floor. A swimming fish girl immediately appeared on the arched ceiling above her, only this one had dark hair braided just like her own. Kiri realized the swimming girl was supposed to resemble her, except it looked brighter and prettier than her, with a happy smile on her flawless face and a pink fish tail instead of legs. Seeing her vid image on the ceiling made Kiri feel even more trapped, as if the vids knew exactly where she was going and what she would do.

She sped up in an attempt to lose her sea person self. Kiri tried jogging, then running, then sprinting. The moving floor added to her speed, but the faster she went, the faster her smiling fish self swam.

She passed a hall with mostly purple fish, and another full of red fish. Then she darted into a yellow fish hall, but her stupid, smiling sea person stayed with her, not falling even an inch behind. At one point, she almost slammed into a man in a green coat who had stepped out of a room ahead of her.

"Slow down!" he snapped. "This isn't a gym."

The sea person on the ceiling right above him waved and smiled at Kiri. But the man in the green coat didn't smile at all.

Kiri dashed down another hall in case the man tried to drag her back to her room, but he just stared at a screen in his hand and let the floor carry him away.

The hall she'd entered must have been the main one, because it was wider and busier than the others. Several halls branched off it, each looking like the one she'd left. The only difference was that the fish were different colors in each hall. Kiri searched for a window or a door that led outside. She couldn't find any.

Her chest tightened and pulse raced. Never in her life had she been in a building this big—so big that Kiri wondered if it had eaten everything else, like a greedy snake that couldn't stop swallowing things. *Maybe nothing outside exists anymore.*

She shook her head to clear it. There had to be a

window or exit somewhere—a way to step outside and smell the air, and to see what the waller city really looked like. She might be able to see where the panther cubs were, too. Wallers couldn't live inside surrounded by vid screens all the time, could they?

Kiri tried to calm down, but the more she searched, the more she realized that the main hall just curved around in one giant circle, without windows or exits or end. She wanted to scream, only she could barely breathe. There didn't seem to be enough air in the hallway anymore. *I have to get out!* she thought, her breath coming in short, panicked gasps.

She darted down the red fish hall, not knowing where she was going—just knowing she needed to escape this place. One of the doors ahead suddenly gaped open and Squirrel Woman's sea person appeared on the ceiling.

Afraid she'd be caught and locked in her room, Kiri pushed open the closest door and ducked inside.

The room looked the same as hers, except flying lizards frolicked on the ceiling instead of kittens, and the bed was crowded with bright blankets and stuffed animals. A table next to the bed had several models of tall buildings on it. Also, the bed was bent in the middle, so the person in it was able to sit upright while lying back.

The bed's occupant glanced up from the vid screen he held. His pale face, though young, appeared surprisingly hairless. Even his eyebrows were gone, and he didn't seem to have eyelashes either. Without hair, his round head resembled an egg with eyes drawn on it.

Kiri startled at the strange sight.

The egg-headed boy seemed equally astonished by her. He stared for a long, quiet moment. Then his cheeks dimpled and his lips curved up in a lopsided grin.

"Hello," he said. "You're not supposed to be here, are you?"

# -22-

## The Cosmic Fingernail

Kiri stood, too afraid to speak. If the boy called for help, Squirrel Woman would find her.

She scanned the room for another exit, but the only way out was the way she'd come in. The boy seemed younger than her, maybe nine or ten, although the corners of his eyes were wrinkled like an old man's. Still, his arms were skinnier than hers, and his neck looked stick thin.

"It's all right," he said. "I like visitors. What are you sick with?"

"Nothing. I'm fine." Kiri glanced at the door, afraid that Squirrel Woman would hear them talking.

The boy didn't seem the least bit concerned about being overheard. "Liar," he said. "Why are you wearing a hospital gown if you're not sick?"

"They put it on me."

He cocked his head. "You talk funny."

"So do you," replied Kiri, searching the room again for an exit. Her heart kept pounding in her chest.

"Nuh-uh. I have a perfectly normal accent. It's how vid casters speak." He pulled the table next to his bed closer and fidgeted with some of the miniature buildings. "Do you like models?" he asked, holding up a tall, pointy one. "I build them and paint them. Then I dress my stuffed animals up like monsters and destroy the buildings."

It had been Kiri's intention to leave the room as soon as the hallway was clear, but she still had no idea where to go and she found the boy's friendly tone to be unexpectedly calming. The panic she'd felt in the hallway started to ease. Without meaning to, she stepped closer to look at the models. Some reminded her of the ruins, only much taller and not ruined. There were doors, ledges, windows, and other tiny details painted on them with incredible care. Kiri figured it must have taken the boy a long time to create them, and for what? To destroy them with a stuffed animal?

"Why?" she asked.

"For a vid, of course." He nodded to his vid screen. "I make vids. Basho thrasher ones. On-screen it looks like a monster bunny is crushing everything. Funny, huh? I made one vid of a baby zombie panda destroying my school. You don't have cancer, do you?"

Kiri cocked her head, perplexed by the strange boy's questions.

"You don't," decided the boy. "This is the cancer ward. All the kids here have cancer and lose their hair, but you have plenty of hair. Still, you've been scratched by the cosmic fingernail. I can tell."

"The cosmic what?"

"The cosmic fingernail. It scratched you," said the boy. He leaned forward and touched the scar on her cheek. "Right there!"

The devi mark on Kiri's cheek tingled. She'd expected the boy's finger to be cold, like everything else here, but it wasn't. His touch felt surprisingly warm, and that warmth spread through her.

She stepped back, startled, and felt the scar on her cheek. "This is from a sea turtle bone," she said.

"A bone might have *made* the cut, but the cosmic fingernail *caused* it," replied the boy. "My mom says that sometimes, when the cosmic fingernail scratches you, it's because the cosmic hand is giving you something. It hurts, but the deeper the scratch, the more it gives you."

Kiri studied the boy, wondering if he knew anything about sea turtles and devi. "What does it give you?" she asked.

"A glow—that's what it looks like to me. And yours is bright violet and pretty," said the boy. "I only like talking to people who've been scratched by the cosmic fingernail. They're more interesting than ordinary people. I have a few friends at school who've never been scratched at all and they're very boring. But you're not like that. Not in the least."

"How do you know?"

"I told you, I have a sense about these things. I'm Apson, by the way." The boy thrust a bony hand toward her. "Everyone calls me Ap because of my name, and because I scored highest on my school's aptitude tests. All that means, though, is that I have to do more homeschool problems. You can call me Ap, too."

Kiri stared at his hand.

"It's okay. I'm not contagious," said Ap. "It's the chemicals in the water that made me sick. That's what my father says, but the city officials don't believe him."

The boy kept holding his hand out until Kiri raised her own hand to shake his. Even though he was a waller and the strangest person she'd ever met, she felt at ease around him.

His smile widened as he took her hand and shook it up and down in greeting. "There. Now we're friends and you can come back to my room anytime and we can play *Toxic War Toads*. But if a nurse catches you here, you'll get a demerit and you won't be able to go to the treasure chest. I don't care about the treasure chest, though. I've been here so long that I already have every stuffed animal. See?" He nodded to the foot of his bed, where dozens of fuzzy creatures were arranged.

One of the stuffed animals was yellow with a long, spotted neck and thin legs. Another resembled an orange cat with black stripes. There was also a white horse with a horn in the center of its head, and a tawny, big-pawed cat that reminded Kiri of the panther cubs.

*Once-were creatures,* she thought. *They're all once-were creatures.*

"You can take one if you like," said Ap.

Kiri picked up a small green creature with blue plastic eyes, a soft round head, four floppy legs, and a smooth brown shell on its back. It reminded her of the leatherback turtle Charro had netted.

"That's Bodhi," said Ap. "Go on, take him. He'll bring you good luck."

Kiri stuffed the little cloth turtle into her pocket, grateful to have this reminder of the ocean. "Thank you."

"I've made vids of them destroying all sorts of things," said Ap. "I make lots of vids because I don't have to go to school. That's the best part of being sick, don't you think?"

"I wouldn't know. I've never been to school."

Ap's eyes widened. Kiri supposed, if he'd had eyebrows, they would have been raised, but all that happened was his forehead wrinkled.

"You've *never* gone to school?"

"Nope."

"That's flip!" His missing eyebrows shot up even farther, adding another wrinkle to his forehead. "You must be very sick. What do you do all day?"

Kiri squeezed the stuffed turtle in her pocket, picturing what her life had been like before she'd been brought here. She desperately wanted to smell the ocean again. Not the claustrophobic fake ocean in the hallway, but the real ocean, with its seaweed, stinging jellies, and crashing waves. "I go to the beach to collect samples for my da," she said. "And I dig for sand fleas, and fish, and get palm nuts for Snowflake, my rat. At least, I used to."

"Wow. You're really off ward," said Ap.

"Off *ward*?"

"You know, the part of the facility where you're supposed to be."

Kiri recalled Sonia mentioning a ward when she'd talked about the panther cubs. "Do you know where the animal ward is?"

"I know everything here. And you don't—I see that now. Are you even from this city?"

"Not exactly."

"I knew it! You're from one of the floating cities, aren't you? I saw a vid about them. They're like big square boats, and the ground constantly moves up and down. And they have buildings that go underwater like skyscrapers in reverse, with tubes that connect them—just like the vista screens in the hallway, only real."

"I'm not from any city," said Kiri.

"You have to be from some city. Everyone's from a city."

"I'm not."

Ap looked perplexed. Did he even know that fugees existed?

"Then where do you live?" he asked.

Kiri opened her mouth to respond, but no words came out. Where *did* she live now? She couldn't go back to the swamp, and she might never be able to return to the fugee village. "I don't know," she said. "Nowhere, I guess."

"That means you're No Name from No Where!" said Ap. "Because you didn't tell me your name before."

Kiri smiled despite herself. She considered telling Ap her name. He was the first person she'd met here whom she felt comfortable talking to. In fact, now that she thought about it, there *did* seem to be a sort of inviting glow around him, so maybe he'd been scratched by the cosmic fingernail, too.

Ap pushed a button that made his bed tilt up farther. Then he folded down the railing, swung his feet off the bed, and nudged a chair with wheels on it toward him with his foot. His legs were as skinny as a bird's.

"You can push me to the hall," he said once he'd slid into the wheeled chair. "Put that on," he added, pointing to a blue coat hanging on a hook. "That way people will think you're a visitor and not a patient who's gone off ward and needs a demerit. Now, let's go."

"Go where?" asked Kiri.

"To the animal ward. That's what you wanted to find, right?"

🐢

They drifted on the track to the main hallway. Ap's sea person looked huge and ridiculously muscular compared with him. It was funny seeing such a big, strong figure swim above the small, frail boy in the wheeled chair.

"I reprogrammed it," said Ap, nodding to the sea person above him. "He's the biggest avatar in the facility."

Ap's sea person grinned and waved at everyone they

passed, but none of the real doctors and nurses said anything. Everyone appeared too busy to notice them. On the
bright side, no one seemed to care that they were out wan-
dering the halls.

They entered a small metal room off the main hall with
shiny doors that slid open and closed on their own.

"Most of the upper levels are people wards," said Ap.
"The cool stuff is all underground. That's where they do
research. Levels N4 through N7 are contagious disease
wards, so we can't go there. I bet it's N3." He pushed a
button on the wall.

The metal room seemed to drop out from under them.
Kiri scrambled for something to hold on to, but Ap wasn't
the least bit alarmed. After several seconds of falling, the
room stopped moving and the door opened. The floor didn't
move, so Kiri pushed Ap's wheeled chair into a short, plain
hallway that ended at a set of locked double doors. ANIMAL
WARD B was written on a red sign above the doors.

"Told you I knew everything," said Ap. "Now what?"

"Now we go in." Kiri tried to push open the doors, but
they were locked.

"Typical," said Ap. "Let's go to the elder ward. They
have a game room with total immersion bubble screens.
It's flip, although the controllers are sticky."

Kiri noticed a keypad next to the doors, like the one
that had been on the machine behind her bed. She punched
in the code the nurse had used.

3-6-9-3

The doors swung open.

"Basho!" said Ap, raising his nonexistent eyebrows again.

The hall on the other side was dull and sterile, with bright overhead lights and no vid images on the walls, but it smelled completely different. Beneath the usual fake-flowery scent were wild, lush, animal smells—hair, dirt, blood, and cedar, all mixed together, with the lingering odor of ammonia and dung.

A rush of air pushed Kiri's hair back as she walked through the doors. Then came a cacophony of chirps, mews, and barks. There was music being piped in, too—wordless waller music, like the sort her da listened to.

"Wow! Chickens!" said Ap, pointing to a sign on one door. "And bunnies!" he added, pointing to another door across the hallway. "I've never seen a real bunny. Or a chicken."

A man dressed head to toe in a white hooded jumpsuit spotted them. "This is a restricted area. You're not allowed here."

Kiri looked at Ap. He'd tensed and gone quiet, just like she had when the floor had dropped in the metal room. She knew he was scared, but this might be their only chance.

"I'm here to see the panther cubs," she said with every ounce of authority she could muster.

The man straightened. "How do you know about those?"

"Because they're mine. I'm the one who found them," said Kiri.

More people drifted into the hall from the same direction the man had come.

"Kiribati?" said one figure. It wasn't until he tugged off the white hood covering his head that Kiri recognized her da. "You shouldn't be here. This area's strictly off-limits."

"It's all right, Martin," said a smaller figure. She pushed back her hood and a cascade of dark, curly hair sprang out. "She can stay," said Sonia. "Isn't it time she learned what you really do?"

# −23−

# Wolves in the Valley

A nurse came to escort Ap back to his room. Kiri didn't want him to go. Even though she'd known him only a short time, she already considered him a friend—the only friend she had here.

Before Ap left, he took Kiri's hand and squinted at her, as if trying to figure something out. "I'll see you again," he determined. Then the nurse wheeled him away.

"Some of us refer to this as 'the Ark,'" said Sonia, after the door clicked shut behind Ap. "I prefer to think of it as a seed bank for a better future."

As Sonia talked, she led Kiri and Martin down the hall. They passed rooms from which various animal smells and sounds emerged—cedar shavings and the musk of damp fur colliding with chickens clucking and the distant echo of a dog barking.

"There's a story I often think about that helps explain the importance of the work we're doing at Gen Tech. Would you like to hear it?" asked Sonia.

Kiri studied the doors they passed for clues of what might be on the other side. Each door was labeled with a single, strange word. Kiri struggled to read them.

CANIDAE.

RANIDAE.

DIPODIDAE.

CEBIDAE.

NATALIDAE.

A few doors had small windows that Kiri glanced through, but all she saw were labs full of vid screens and other equipment.

"It's a true story, about a place called Yellowstone," continued Sonia. "It was a very large, beautiful wilderness area that people traveled from all over the world to see. There were mountains, rivers, valleys, and wetlands there, but despite all the protected land and species, the wilderness was dying. Beetles were killing the pines, and deer overgrazed the valleys. Severe fires swept through the park more frequently, and the ground began to wash away, clogging the rivers with mud. Then the trout began to disappear, as well as animals that fed on trout. The entire ecosystem spiraled toward collapse. You see, the wilderness was missing one thing—an apex predator. In this case, wolves." Sonia paused and turned to Kiri. "Do you know what a wolf is?"

"I read stories about them in a book my da gave me," said Kiri. "They were always the villains."

Martin chuckled. He'd been silent for most of the walk, drifting back and letting Sonia do the talking, but now he spoke. "Those were just fairy tales, Kiribati."

"I know that," said Kiri. "But that was the only book we had on wolves."

"It'll do," said Sonia. "One thing fairy tales show is how much people feared wolves." She slowed and cocked her head at Kiri. "Did you know that wolves once roamed this whole continent? They were everywhere, but when settlers first arrived, they saw wolves as their enemies so they tried to hunt and poison them to extinction. Only a small number of wolves survived. Then a few people, scientists mostly, thought it might be good to reintroduce wolves to some of the habitats where they'd once lived."

Sonia continued down another hall lined with doors. "By this point, there weren't many wilderness areas left that could sustain even a small wolf pack. One such place, though, was Yellowstone."

"The beautiful, dying wilderness," said Kiri, to show that she'd been paying attention.

"Yes." Sonia smiled at her. "It was an experiment. No one knew what would happen when wolves returned. Some thought they'd kill too many deer. Others thought the wolves would leave the area and prey on livestock. Despite all the opposition, a small breeding population was eventually released. And what happened next, in just a few years, surprised everyone."

Sonia paused, letting the suspense grow. Her dark brown eyes seemed to sparkle. Kiri realized that her voice had changed as well, becoming more lilting and musical as she'd gotten into the story. "The wolves not only hunted deer," she said, "they set off a trophic cascade that changed the entire ecosystem and reshaped the land itself. Rivers deepened, valleys shifted, and wetlands formed— mostly due to the wolf's return."

"How?" asked Kiri, unable to picture how wolves could change rivers and valleys.

"Good question," said Sonia. "The wolves only ate a small percentage of deer in the area, but their presence caused all the herds to move about more to avoid the wolves, and so the deer and elk didn't overgraze areas as they'd done before. As a result, trees that had been stunted by grazing began to grow tall and strong. And the roots of these trees stabilized the earth and prevented dirt from washing into the rivers. Then the rivers ran deeper and clearer, which was what the trout needed to thrive. And as the rivers deepened and the trees grew, beavers and birds came back." Sonia looked up, as if she could see the creatures she talked about. "The beavers created dams that led to wetlands where more fish and birds could live. Then hawks, owls, and eagles returned, along with minks, fishers, and otters—"

"What are those?" asked Kiri, not recognizing half the animals Sonia had named.

"They're . . . *once-were* creatures," said Martin.

Sonia nodded and turned down another hall. "Suffice it to say, the more species that returned, the healthier the wilderness became. Even the deer became healthier because the wolves preyed on the sick. You see? In just a few decades, the entire landscape was more stable, diverse, and abundant, all because one critical species had returned."

"Then what happened?" asked Kiri.

"Well . . ." Sonia glanced at Martin.

"Other factors impacted the area, Kiribati," said her da. "Most of the species in that wilderness have since died off."

"Why?"

Her da shrugged. "Pollution increased. The climate changed. Pollinators disappeared. Toxins accumulated. . . . There are only so many stressors an ecosystem can take before it collapses."

"The point of my story," said Sonia, "is that every species is connected to other species *and* to the land itself in ways we barely understand. Losing just a few key species can cause the whole web to unravel. And that's where we are now—in the midst of the largest die-off of species since the dinosaurs were wiped out sixty-five million years ago. Only now we're the cause. We're driving much of life on Earth to extinction."

Sonia stopped in front of a door marked FELIDAE. "That's why the work we're doing here—the work your father is doing—is so incredibly important. He's not just collecting specimens. He's helping preserve entire ecosystems for the future. If we're going to have any hope of stopping a catastrophic collapse, we need to save all the species we can. Especially apex predators." She pressed her palm to a panel next to the door and stared at a lens set into the wall. Then, in a stiff voice that had no trace of her musical, storytelling cadence, she said, "Sonia Waterson entering with two guests."

The door clicked open and Sonia led them into a narrow room lined with cabinets. "Gen Tech is racing to collect and preserve as many species as possible before they're gone," she said. "It's our hope that by retrieving viable numbers of rare specimens, we might be able to reintroduce populations to the wild someday."

"Like they did with the wolves?" Kiri asked.

"Precisely," said Sonia. "The trouble is, for most of the species we collect, there simply aren't suitable wilderness areas left where we could reintroduce them."

"What about the panther cubs? Are you still keeping them here?"

"For now. Would you like to see them?"

Kiri's heart skipped. She nodded, too excited to speak.

Sonia held her hand before a sensor near a door at the far end of the room. There was a rush of air as the door slid open, then Sonia led Kiri and her da into a dimly lit corridor with a broad wall made of glass.

Kiri ran to the glass wall. Below stretched an enclosure that resembled the ghost forest. Several clumps of saw palms dotted the sandy floor. A small pool occupied the center, and stands of cypress and pine trees grew in the distance. Unlike the underwater images in the hallways, the enclosure on the other side appeared to be real.

Kiri spotted movement in front of a concrete den covered in palm fronds. One of the panther cubs was playing with a pink stuffed bunny, rolling on his back while clasping the stuffed animal between his forepaws, then throwing it off and pouncing on it with a curious, high hop.

"That's Cricket!" Kiri gasped. Relief at seeing the cub again took Kiri's breath away.

"*Cricket?*" repeated her da. "You named him that?"

Kiri nodded. "Because he likes to hop."

"I see," said her da, sounding amazed. "Kiribati, your mother used to call *you* Cricket."

"I know," she said, not daring to take her eyes off the cub.

Another small bundle of speckled fur emerged from the den to join the game, only this one was more hesitant. She stayed low and crawled toward the pink bunny as if trying to sneak up on it, before retreating with several quick, dainty steps.

"There's Skitter! Little Skitter!" exclaimed Kiri, pointing at the nervous cub.

She glanced around for the third cub, suddenly worried that he might not have made it. Then Kiri spotted him on top of the concrete den. His dusky fur blended in perfectly with the shadows of the palm fronds. Only his yawn gave him away, and the characteristic dark line across his muzzle. "And Mustache! He's the lazy one."

"Good names," replied Sonia. "Much better than the ones we've been using for them. Right, Jackson?"

A man taking notes on a vid screen at the far end of the observation room nodded. "PC-12 doesn't have the same ring to it as Cricket," he said.

"All three of them were malnourished when we brought them in," explained Sonia. "The mother must have run out of milk. That's probably why she risked venturing so close to the refugee village. Normally, *Puma concolor* are far more wary and elusive."

Skitter finally got over her fear and pounced on the pink bunny, but as soon as it fell over, she jumped back and scampered into the den. Mustache stretched and turned his back on the commotion, annoyed.

"For a while we didn't know if PC-13—the one you named Skitter—would survive," continued Sonia. "She seemed the weakest of the three. But now she's gaining weight. With the genetic diversity these three provide, we might be able to breed them with samples from other sub-species someday. That's why we're grateful that you found them. These cubs could preserve the genetic line of one of the most magnificent apex predators we've ever known." Sonia turned to regard Kiri. "Now do you see why they're so important to us?"

"I think so," said Kiri.

"Excellent. Because we have good news for you." Sonia gave Martin a long look.

Finally, her da spoke. "Sonia thinks we can use the

value of the cubs to negotiate with the city officers for citizenship."

"Citizenship?"

"For you," said her da. "You'll be able to stay in the city then. We both can. We'll be assigned an apartment in the science complex."

"You'll have to go to school, of course," added Sonia, standing next to her da.

"But I think you'll like it," said Martin. "You'll get to learn about many wonderful things, and you'll be able to play with other kids your age. We won't have to worry about being hungry anymore, either. Or getting sick, or storms, snakes, mosquitoes . . . You might even get your own room. How's that sound?"

Kiri tried to picture the life her da had just described. He talked about it like it was a good thing, only she couldn't imagine living in the city, away from the forest and the ocean. The devi mark on her shoulder began to tingle and itch in a way it hadn't in days. "What about the cubs?" she asked, rubbing the mark on her shoulder. "Will I get to see them?"

"You might be able to visit them," said her da, glancing at Sonia.

"I don't see why not," agreed Sonia. "I could talk with the head zoologist about making you an assistant caretaker. Then you could drop by after school and learn how to care for them."

"Here?" asked Kiri.

"This is where they'll be," said Sonia. She brushed

back the braids on the side of Kiri's head. "We'll all be together."

Kiri studied Sonia, struck by the familiarity of the gesture. "Are you the one who braided my hair?"

Sonia nodded. "Many different people live in the city, Kiri, but we're all citizens. We all call it home. It could be your home, too."

Kiri wondered if that was true. Could this place ever be her home?

The thought of living in the endless claustrophobic halls terrified her. Maybe it wasn't all like that, though. After all, the cubs seemed fine. They weren't in danger like she'd feared. So maybe other things weren't as bad as she thought. There had to be windows somewhere, and places where she could go outside. And there seemed to be good people here, too, like Ap and Sonia. People who might accept her. She could be friends with Ap, and work with her da, and look after the cubs like she'd promised the panther mother she'd do. And the cubs did seem safe here. At least they looked healthy and well fed. Staying might be good for them.

"Hey," said her da. "Once I save up enough credits, we can even get that scar removed."

Kiri realized she was touching the devi mark on her cheek. It had started to tingle and itch as well. She thought about the bone that had caused it, and how the magnificent sea turtle had gazed longingly toward the ocean waves as it was being pulled to shore. She felt a longing like that now, as if she were caught in a net and being dragged in.

She peered down at the cubs in the enclosure. Cricket had moved to the edge of the forest beyond the den. He clawed at the base of a tree. But it wasn't a tree. It was a vid screen wall. He frantically scraped his claws against it, as if trying to tear it down, only his claws kept sliding off the glass.

The walls surrounding the enclosure may have looked like forests, but they weren't forests. They were walls, and the cubs weren't fooled by the pretty pictures of trees and grass that they showed. Even from up on the balcony overlooking the enclosure, Kiri could sense the cubs' anxiety. She could feel it in the way her devi marks throbbed and itched, and in the way her chest ached. The cubs may have been healthy and well fed, yet something was missing. Something they desperately needed. They wanted out of here, just like she wanted out of here.

*No wall can stop the unraveling,* she thought, recalling the warning that her mother had given her.

Dragging the sea turtle to shore, trapping the panther, keeping the cubs here—it all led to the same thing. It cut them off from the life they'd been part of, and the life they'd been part of would be lost as well.

"No," she decided. "It won't work. We can't stay here."

"Of course we can," said her da. "This is where we belong now."

"*They* don't belong here." Kiri nodded to the cubs. "It's like the story of the wolves—if you take them away, everything unravels."

"Sweetie, I know what you're thinking," said Sonia. "You want them to be free. So do I. Believe me, I wish there was a place where we could release them, but that's simply not feasible right now. Even fully grown, these cubs can't live in the wild. You saw what happened. The refugees were going to hunt them and sell them on the black market, and Gen Tech doesn't have the resources to keep them safe outside the city walls."

"Besides, we need the cubs to get you citizenship," explained her da. "It's not safe on the coast anymore—not for you or them."

"But they need to go back. *We* need to go back," said Kiri.

"The cubs are staying here, Kiribati, and so are we," replied her da.

"So that's it?" Kiri couldn't believe her da wouldn't listen to her. He wasn't even trying to understand. "I'm just supposed to stay here and never see the fugee village again? Or the ocean? Or any of it?"

"We have really good oceanscapes on file," offered Sonia.

"Vids!" said Kiri, furious that Sonia would even suggest such a thing. Vids weren't real, and they made everything else seem less real too. "You better not turn my beach into a vid."

"Kiribati!" scolded her da.

But Kiri was too upset to calm down. "What about Paulo? Will I ever get to see him again?"

Her da clenched his jaw and fidgeted with his white jumpsuit.

"Can I at least say goodbye to Paulo?"

"We do have to return to collect supplies . . . ," hedged Sonia.

"It's too dangerous," said Martin.

"Please! I just want to see Paulo one last time."

Martin looked from Sonia to Kiri. At last he sighed, giving in. "Fine. You can come with us to say goodbye, but don't expect too much. Your friend might not want to see you."

Kiri drew back, stung by her father's words.

"I wish the world were a different place, Kiribati," he added in a softer voice. "A world more like the one you imagine, where we could release the cubs and all live peacefully together without walls. But that's not the world we live in. It's time you realize that. If people could change, they would have changed long ago when it first became clear how we were throwing things out of balance. Only people didn't change then, and they won't change now, no matter how much you might want them to."

Kiri looked away and shoved her hands into her pockets. She felt the soft shell of the stuffed turtle Ap had given her. Her da was wrong. He had to be. People could change. Things could be different.

Childish as it might seem, she refused to let go of hope.

# —24—

## The Return of a Ghost

Dozens of villagers poured onto the beach. It was midday, so most of the netters were in, waiting for the tide to turn and the heat to slacken. By the time the pilot set the tridrone down on a patch of sand near the sea-grape tunnels, about a hundred fugees had gathered. They peered at the huge black tridrone with their hands clasped over their faces to shelter their eyes from the blowing sand.

Through a vid screen window inside the tridrone, Kiri saw Charro standing among the villagers, long gun clutched in his hands. He wasn't pointing the black barrel at them, but he wasn't lowering it either. That had the soldiers in the cargo bay anxious. As soon as the skids touched the ground, the soldiers rushed out the back ramp with their waller guns raised.

*"Put your weapons down!"* shouted the soldiers as they took up positions around the tridrone.

All four soldiers wore flex armor that covered everything, even their faces, and the waller guns they carried looked large and deadly.

Charro glared at the soldiers, his expression full of contempt.

Martin went out, despite Sonia's protests, to try to calm the situation. Kiri listened to his muffled voice through the metal walls of the tridrone as he told the fugees they were only returning to pick up the equipment he'd left behind and to take down portions of the fence. "It's a peaceful mission," he said. "As long as we aren't threatened, no harm will come to you."

Without a word, Charro turned and walked back to the village. Most of the netters went with him. A moment later, all the fugees turned their backs on Martin and shuffled to the village in silence, as if Martin and the waller soldiers weren't even there.

"We're clear and secure!" shouted the lead soldier.

Sonia helped Kiri unbuckle her safety harness. "I know it's hard to say goodbye. Just remember, you have a wonderful new life ahead of you."

Kiri didn't say anything in response. She didn't want a new life—at least, not one in the walled-off city with its vid screen tunnels and kitten-cloud skies.

She hurried out the back ramp and onto the beach. It wasn't perfect, but it was real. The salty seaweed smell of the ocean and the slap of the too-bright sun made her heart soar.

"See your friend?" asked Martin.

Kiri stared at the village. She saw a few figures move between stilt houses, only she couldn't recognize them. No one in the village even seemed willing to look her way. At the very least she'd thought Paulo might wave to her, yet no one did. She was dead to them.

"Sorry, Kiribati," said her da. "I feared it might be like this."

Her gaze fell. She was wearing shoes—the sort of thick-soled shoes that wallers wore—so the ground felt dull. "It's nice to see the beach again."

Martin nodded. "Stay here with the pilot. We're leaving two guards to keep watch over the tridrone. The other two are going with us to help carry back equipment. Is there anything from the house you'd like me to get?"

The only thing Kiri had left from her life before that mattered to her was Snowflake, but she doubted he'd be at the stilt house in the swamp. And even if he was, she didn't think her da would let her take a rat back to the city. That was assuming Snowflake would *want* to come with her, which he probably wouldn't. This was his home.

All her other possessions were things wallers would consider junk—old ripped clothes and a collection of sea glass, shells, and driftwood that she'd found over the years. Stuff that would look dirty and pointless in the city. The one possession she wanted to keep was her mother's knife, and she already had that with her, strapped to her belt and hidden beneath her shirt. Her hand went to it now, touching the worn handle. Then her fingers drifted to the stuffed turtle in her pocket. She pressed the soft, round shell against her leg for reassurance. "No," she told her da. "Leave it all."

Martin kissed her forehead and set off with Sonia and two of the soldiers. Kiri watched them go. Once they passed through the sea-grape tunnels, she pried off her shoes so she could feel the sand between her toes one last time.

The soldiers paid her no mind. They both stood in the shade of the tridrone, scanning the dunes.

A skinny figure paused beneath a stilt house at the back edge of the village. He blended in with the wooden stilts, but the funny way he held his shoulders and cocked his head were unmistakable.

*Paulo!*

Instinctively, Kiri jogged toward him.

"Hey!" shouted a soldier. "Get back here!"

"It's okay," she called back. "I'm going to talk with a friend."

She feared the soldiers might come after her, but they didn't. They probably thought fugees were all crazy savages who'd net them and eat them if they went anywhere near the village. And they probably considered her a crazy savage, too. After a few sharp commands, they let her go.

As Kiri neared the stilt house at the edge of the village, she saw that she'd been right. It *was* Paulo standing in the shade under the house. Only he wasn't smiling. Instead, he looked scared.

"Paulo!"

He grimaced and turned his back to her.

"Paulo! It's me."

"You shouldn't be here," he said, still refusing to look at her. "You're dead. I saw you get shot. Everyone says that you're dead."

"If I was dead, could I do this?" Kiri picked up a clump of rotting seaweed and threw it at his back.

The seaweed hit him with a wet thump and rolled off his hoodie. Only it wasn't *his* hoodie. It was hers—one she'd left behind. The hood began to shift and change shape. A moment later a pink nose emerged, followed by a brown and white head.

*"Snowflake?"*

The little rat climbed onto Paulo's shoulder and squeaked in response.

Kiri hurried closer, but Paulo edged away. "I'm not supposed to talk with you," he said, voice wavering. "How do I know you're not a ghost?"

"Snowflake knows." Kiri reached her hand out to the little rat. Snowflake trembled and spun in fast little circles on Paulo's shoulder, like he wanted to be mad at Kiri, but he was too happy to see her again to stay still. Suddenly, he leapt onto Kiri's hand and scrambled up her arm to her shoulder, where he started to lick her cheek and nuzzle her ear while squeaking.

"It's good to see you, too, Snowflake," said Kiri, giggling as the rat's whiskers tickled her face.

She lifted him off her shoulder and cradled him in her hands, rubbing her nose against his.

Snowflake kept sniffing and squeaking softly.

"Never seen him do that before," admitted Paulo, finally cracking a smile. "I guess he does know."

"Where'd you find him?"

"At your house. The day after they took you, I found him in the loft, curled up on your hoodie. He wouldn't eat. I couldn't get him to eat for days. He cried tears of blood."

"Rats do that when they're sad," said Kiri. She kissed the star on Snowflake's head, breathing in his familiar pine-bark-and-coconut smell. He must have scampered back to the house after she'd left him in the ghost forest. It couldn't have been an easy journey for him. "I missed you, too, Snowflake."

"Here." Paulo took off the sleeveless hoodie and handed it to her. "I borrowed this."

Kiri let Snowflake climb into the hood, then she pulled the hoodie on over her waller clothes. Snowflake's paws against her neck sent joyful shivers through her. "Thank you, Paulo. You're a good friend. I was afraid he'd get eaten."

"I considered it, but he's skinnier than he looks," joked Paulo. "Besides, he had no other place to go, which makes him a fugee like me. And fugees always look out for each other."

Another shiver coursed through Kiri, only this time it

didn't come from Snowflake's tickling paws. "What did you say?" she asked, getting the first flicker of an idea.

"Just that fugees always look out for each other. It's what we do. That's why I went to your place to search for him."

"Paulo, that's it! You're brilliant!"

"Well, yeah. I mean, duh . . ." He paused. "What did I say that's brilliant?"

"We have to hurry. I don't have much time. Will you help me?"

"Sure. As long as you're not dead."

Kiri checked to make sure no one else in the village had seen her talking with Paulo. Fortunately, the house they stood beneath was set back from most of the village and sheltered by a dune. "I need you to gather everyone. Tell them to meet in the mending tent. Say one of the elders called a gathering."

"What are you going to do?" asked Paulo.

"I'm going to remind them of what it means to be a fugee."

Paulo looked skeptical. "People don't want to see you, Kiri. They're already angry, and you're not supposed to be here—"

"I know. But I have a plan. Now go! Get everyone."

After Paulo left, Kiri ran to another stilt house at the edge of the village, near the sea-grape tunnels.

The house of the Witch Woman.

# —25—

## Devi Marks

Paulo must have come up with a good lie, because an hour later almost all of the village had gathered at the mending tent. It was no small feat to get so many fugees to come out during the hottest hours of the day.

"Who called this meeting?" demanded Elder Tomas. His bald head glistened with sweat as he settled into his high-backed seat in the center of the tent.

"You did," said a few council members.

"I did no such thing. What's going on here?"

"I called the gathering," announced Kiri. She'd been sitting in the shadows at the edge of the tent with her hood pulled low over her face and Snowflake curled in her lap.

People seemed shocked to see her. They stepped back, giving her plenty of space. Kiri had hoped for as much.

If others thought she was a ghost, like Paulo had, they wouldn't get in her way. She strode toward the center of the gathering with Snowflake on her shoulder.

Elder Tomas leaned forward in his chair and steadied himself with the golden python staff. Charro, Tarun, Senek, and Rifat sat in a semicircle on each side of him.

"Waller Girl," Charro grumbled from his spot closest to Elder Tomas. "I thought we were rid of you."

"I'm no waller," said Kiri, doing her best to keep the tremble in her chest from showing in her voice.

"You're no fugee, either," replied Charro. "You're not welcome here."

"You can't kick out a ghost," said Kiri.

Several people murmured, but Charro merely scowled. "You're no ghost. Any fool with eyes can see you're just a greedy waller child who keeps causing trouble."

"You said the fever would kill me, Charro. Maybe it did."

"Someone shut her up before I do," muttered Charro. "This *child* has no right to speak here."

"She has every right," said the Witch Woman. Heads turned to watch as the elderly woman made her way to the center of the tent and stood next to Kiri. "She's been marked by three devi. They chose her to be their messenger, so we'd best listen to what she has to say."

"Devi? What devi?" asked Charro.

"You know what devi. That's the mark of a water devi on her cheek," said the Witch Woman, pointing to the scar on Kiri's cheek from where the leatherback bone had scratched her. "And a devi of the land marked her shoulder." The Witch Woman tugged Kiri's hood aside and directed her to turn so everyone could see the raised lines of the panther scratches on her shoulder.

The devi marks warmed as people stared at them, as if rays of sunlight were shining on her cheek and shoulder. The scars she bore weren't simply wounds from the sea turtle and the panther. They were reminders of her connection to the water and the land.

"You said *three* devi. Where's the third mark?" asked Tarun.

Kiri looked to the Witch Woman. The elder woman urged her on. She lifted her arm and turned it so everyone could see the black lines tattooed there.

"A feather," said Nessa. "It's the mark of a sky devi."

"That's three marks," continued the Witch Woman. "Three devi chose her to be their messenger."

A few people in the crowd nodded, appearing to accept what the Witch Woman said. Then Charro stood and grabbed Kiri's wrist. He took a closer look at the black mark there. "That's no feather. That's a waller mark, and the wallers aren't devi."

People jostled each other to see. Kiri's face burned as fugees stared at the waller mark and whispered. She wanted to lower her arm and hide the black lines, but then the mark on her arm began to tingle, the same as the marks on her cheek and shoulder did.

With that tingling came a new awareness. The wallers

were part of this too, along with the panthers and the fu-gees. Perhaps she'd been marked by each so she could serve as a bridge between them, connecting the wallers in their distant cities to the land, water, and people here.

"I told you before, Charro, devi take many forms," said the Witch Woman. "You saw it yourself—Kiri was on death's shore when the wallers came down from the sky and took her. And now she lives. A miracle like that seems the work of a devi to me."

Fugees murmured in awe, but Charro merely scoffed. "I see no miracle," he said. "All I see is a waller trick." He pointed at the tridrone up the beach. "The wallers stole the panther that was ours. They stole the cubs, too. We could have fed the village for a year off what they were worth, but the wallers took them and left us nothing except a fence that divides our land. And now they've returned with soldiers to take more from us?" He glared at the soldiers standing guard around the tridrone. "We starve because they've poisoned the water and taken all the fish away, and once again they threaten us."

Several netters muttered in agreement. Charro was winning them over, getting them to see things his way. Others began to complain about things the wallers had done. She was losing them.

"You're right to be angry," said Kiri, struggling to be heard over the complaints. "The wallers have taken a lot from you, but if you listen to me there's a way to get back some of what's been lost—"

"We're done listening to wallers," interrupted Senek.

More angry voices followed his, drowning out Kiri's.

"Let her speak!" commanded Elder Tomas. He raised the golden python staff until the crowd grew quiet. "The girl is trouble, I'll grant you that. I'd prefer to be rid of her and the wallers. Nevertheless, the wallers are here and so is she. She's spent time with them, so she might know something of use."

Kiri stepped forward to address the council, but the pressure of so many angry faces made her throat clench. *What am I doing here?* she thought. *I'm just a kid. I'm not even welcome here anymore.*

Her gaze settled on the wrinkled face of the Witch Woman. The elder woman nodded, encouraging her. She'd gone to the Witch Woman for help, and the Witch Woman had done all that she could to get the fugees to listen to her. Now she had to speak. Kiri swallowed and took strength from the tingling marks on her cheek, shoulder, and arm. Whether she'd truly been chosen by devi to be a messenger she couldn't say. But if she didn't speak, far more than her place in the village would be lost.

"I can get the wallers to bring the panther cubs back," she said. Her voice shook. "I'll get them to bring you food and medicine, too. They'll help you stay here and protect you from scav raiders."

"Why would they do that?" asked Elder Tomas. "They never cared about us before. Never lifted a hand to help us, not even when we begged them to."

"They'll do it because they need you to protect the panther cubs," said Kiri. "And the panthers need to live here." She took a deep breath, gaining confidence as she spoke. "The panthers have no place left in the world to go, which means they're refugees, like you. And fugees always look out for each other, right?"

Out of the corner of her eye, she saw Paulo nod.

Kiri explained that the wallers wanted to breed the panthers and release them in the wild, but panthers needed a huge habitat to live in—too big an area for the wallers to watch over. The fugees who lived here could watch over them, though, because they knew this land best. Kiri promised the villagers that if they swore to protect the panthers, the wallers would help them. She spoke in a way she never had before, weaving a delicate web of what could be.

"It has to be everyone," she said. "Everyone needs to agree to protect them."

At first, people were silent. Then a few nodded, as if they could see the future she'd described—one where fugees and wallers worked together to protect the land and the creatures that were part of it. She thought they might actually go along with what she said, until Charro spoke.

"I've heard enough waller lies," he said. "The panther was already ours by rights, and those cubs were ours, too. The wallers stole them from us. And now they want us to help them? I'd rather kiss a snake than trust them." He spat at Kiri's feet and stormed out of the tent.

Senek and several others turned to leave with him. It

was all falling apart. Kiri hadn't been able to persuade anyone.

The Witch Woman gave her a mournful look. "You spoke well, child," she said. "They just weren't ready to hear."

# –26–

# The Knife

Kiri stood in the center of the tent, watching the crowd disperse. For several seconds she couldn't move. Her shoulders slumped and her legs felt as if they were sinking into muck. It was all Charro's fault. People had been willing to listen until he tore down the web she'd woven. He was the key to all this—the one who kept ruining things.

Her hand went to the knife at her belt and her fingers closed around the well-worn hilt.

"Charro!" she yelled as she ran through the crowd. "Hey, Charro!"

Fugees watched, but no one moved to stop her. People shuffled back, fearful of what might happen next.

Charro continued walking to where his skiff had been dragged up onto the beach. He leaned over the railing to grab something. When he turned to face Kiri, the long gun was in his hands.

"Leave," he grumbled. "Go back to your people."

"I did. That's why I'm here."

Charro's eyes twitched. Then he shook his head. "You're one of them now. You've got their mark on your arm, just like your da. Go live in their city and never come back here, *Waller Girl*."

Kiri wanted to be angry at him, but something about Charro's words made her think of the story the Witch Woman had told her earlier that day, when she'd gone to the elder woman's house to ask how she'd come to have her mother's knife. It was a story about her mother's past that her da had never told her. A story no one in the village had ever shared with her.

"I know why you hate wallers so much," said Kiri. "It's because of my ma, isn't it?"

"You don't know anything," snapped Charro.

"I know you loved her."

According to the Witch Woman, when Laria went to live in the swamp with Martin, she left her little brother behind in the stilt village. He was just a kid, and since both their parents were dead, he used to follow her around all the time. But when she left, he felt betrayed. He said he'd never talk to her again.

"She was your sister, and she left you for a waller," continued Kiri. "Then she got sick and the wallers let her die."

Charro clutched the long gun so tight his muscles trembled. "Wallers don't care what happens to any of us. They don't even see us as human."

"I bet you hate her, too, for leaving you," said Kiri. "Is that why you hate me?"

"I don't hate you," he muttered, but he didn't look at her when he said it.

"Am I like her?"

Charro seemed taken aback by the question. He didn't answer right away. Turning, he set the long gun down in the skiff. When next he looked at her, his gaze settled on her hair.

"Your ma had braids like that," he said. "And you're bold and stubborn like her—I'll give you that. But you're not like she was."

Kiri's shoulders slumped. She couldn't help feeling disappointed. "Because of this?" she asked, holding up her arm with the waller mark on it.

"No."

"Then why?"

"Because you came back," said Charro. "She never did. After she left with your da, she never once returned."

Kiri was surprised to hear Charro's voice quaver. She looked at him, but instead of seeing the hard, angry netter, she saw the boy the Witch Woman had described—the scared, lost boy who'd been abandoned by both his parents and his sister. The boy who wanted nothing more than to have a family and a place where he belonged. She knew what that was like. She'd felt that way most of her life.

Perhaps they weren't so different after all, except her ma had come back for her, but not for him.

*Maybe now she can,* thought Kiri.

She pulled the knife from the sheath stitched to her belt. "Here."

Charro stared at the knife. Slowly, his face softened with recognition.

He lifted the knife from her hand and studied the etchings in the blade. "This was our father's knife. It was the only thing Laria took with her when she left."

"Take it," said Kiri, remembering something her ma had said in one of her visions—that a knife wasn't only for cutting but for mending too. Maybe this was what she'd meant. "I think she wanted you to have it."

Charro kept staring at the knife in his hand.

Kiri turned to walk away from the village. Snowflake climbed onto her shoulder and sniffed at her ear as she left. She knew she should take the little rat back to Paulo, only she wasn't ready to say goodbye to him again.

"Wait," called Charro. "Can you really get the wallers to bring back the cubs?"

Kiri slowed. "I think so. If all the fugees swear to protect them."

"I'm not going to let the wallers take any more from us. Understand?"

She nodded.

"All right. I'll do it, then," said Charro. "I'll protect them. And I'll persuade the other netters and council members to do the same, on one condition."

"What?"

"You come out on the skiff with me sometime and help pull in the nets and crab traps," said Charro. "Fair enough?"

"Fair enough," said Kiri, unable to hold back a smile. "Thank you, Uncle."

# -27-

# When the Dead Call

The sun had dipped beneath the tops of the sea-grape dunes when Martin, Sonia, and the two soldiers finally returned carrying packs stuffed with equipment. Kiri had been watching for them. As soon as they got back to the tridrone, she ran down the beach to tell them the good news. Paulo, Tae, and several others trailed after her like the tail of a kite.

The soldiers tensed at the sight of the oncoming mob. Fortunately, Martin recognized Kiri in the lead and ordered the soldiers not to fire. Still, the waller soldiers kept their guns aimed at the approaching villagers. Seeing this, the fugees stopped a good distance from the tridrone.

Kiri went the rest of the way alone, crossing the last open stretch of beach between the fugees and wallers.

"What's going on?" asked Martin. "Why aren't you in the tridrone?"

"They'll do it!" said Kiri. "Everyone in the village swore to protect the cubs. You can bring them back here now, and we can move back with them."

Kiri searched Sonia's and her father's faces, eager to see her own happy expression reflected in theirs, but neither one reacted the way she expected. They both looked tired and gray as the ocean on a day when the sun didn't peek through the clouds.

"Sweetie," said Sonia, "it's a nice idea, but it's not possible."

"But you said you wanted to reintroduce the cubs to the wild. You said you wished there was a place where you could. Now there is. You can turn this whole area into a wilderness refuge and the fugees will watch over it."

"It's not that simple," replied Sonia. "Even if an agreement could be made with the villagers, I'd have to take a proposal to the Gen Tech board, and they'd have to discuss all the variables and do a cost-benefit analysis, not to mention accounting for security risks and insurance for such valuable assets—"

"What are you saying? Are you saying *no*?"

"I'm saying, we can't just get the cubs and release them here."

"Why not? We can build an enclosure near the stilt village and take care of them until they're ready to live on their own."

Sonia sighed and shook her head. "That's not realistic. Gen Tech would never go along with it."

Kiri looked from Sonia to her da. "The cubs need to stay here and everyone needs to work together. Even the marks say so."

Her da looked confused. "What are you talking about, Kiribati?"

"The devi marks," she said. "I understand them now. The first one came from Charro, the second from the panther, and the third from the wallers because they're all part of this."

"Are you feeling all right?" asked her da.

"Don't you see? The wallers and fugees need to work together to make this a refuge," said Kiri. "It's the only way to stop the unraveling. We have to bring the cubs back here."

Martin shook his head. "We can't, Kiribati."

Kiri searched her da's and Sonia's faces again, but neither one seemed about to change their minds.

"It was just a story, wasn't it? You had no intention of ever releasing the cubs, did you?" A storm of dark, twisting feelings churned within her. She'd been a fool to think wallers and fugees could work together. Charro had been right—wallers couldn't be trusted. Her own father couldn't be trusted. He hid behind walls and lied like the rest of them.

"Kiribati, try to understand," said Martin, reaching for her.

But Kiri had heard enough. She ran off.

Her da let her go. He probably thought she'd calm down and forget why she'd been upset. But she wouldn't forget. Not this time.

Paulo and Tae and the others waited for her a couple of skiffs up the beach. If Kiri went to them, they'd ask what had happened and she'd have to explain why everything she'd promised wouldn't happen. They'd hate her and kick her out of the village for good then. She couldn't face that. And she wouldn't return to the waller city, either. She'd never be a waller.

She was no one from nowhere, just like Ap had said.

Kiri ran toward the sea-grape tunnels that led to the ghost forest. Maybe she could go to the stilt house in the swamp and live there with Snowflake. Or she could hide out in the ruins and never speak to anyone again.

At the edge of her vision she saw a shadow move beneath the sea grapes. For a brief moment she thought it might be a panther, but the panthers were all gone—dead or taken away.

She peered into the dark gaps under the red bark branches, unable to shake the sense that someone was there, watching her.

"Ma?" she asked, feeling a faint glimmer of hope. "Is that you?"

Perhaps it had only been leaves swaying in a breeze. Kiri left the path and walked along the edge where the sea grapes met the dunes, searching the shadows under the branches for some sign of where she should go and what she should do.

"Ma, I need you," she said as she approached the area where she'd seen movement. "I tried to tend the tree. I tried to fix things like you said, but nothing worked. No one listened to me."

The shadows didn't respond—not with words or movement. There was nothing but the sound of ocean waves behind her, and wind through the leathery leaves of the sea grapes.

"Please don't be mad at me," she said. "I'm sorry I failed. It was too much. I couldn't change anything."

Still nothing.

Kiri tried to conjure up a specific image of her mother. All she could recall were scenes from different vids her da had shown her. There was the one of her ma holding her when she was only a baby and humming a fugee song to her. Another of her ma catching geckos with her when she was just a curly-haired toddler. And her favorite—a vid of her ma making funny faces and chasing her around the kitchen table while she giggled and ran, looking back every couple of steps to make sure her ma was still there.

"Where are you?" she asked. "I need you."

Kiri searched the darkness under the sea grape branches again. The fronds of a palm tree in the distance looked almost like braids sprouting from the top of her mother's head, cascading around her face. But it wasn't her.

Maybe she'd only seen her mother before because of the fever. She might have just hallucinated her. Or maybe, like the fugee stories of ghosts luring people away from life, she'd only seen her mother's ghost before because she'd been close to dying. *If that's the price, I'll pay it,* thought Kiri.

"Please come back," she said to the shadows. "I miss you so much. I'll go with you now. There's nothing here for me anymore, and I'm not afraid of death, okay? I just want to be with you. So can I be with you now?"

Dry sea-grape leaves rattled in the wind.

Kiri knelt, unable to stand. It was foolish. No one was there. She felt emptier than she had ever been.

Shadows on the sandy ground in front of her began to move. She cocked her head, fearing it might just be a breeze stirring the branches above. But it wasn't—the sand actually moved. Then the earth roiled and shifted, as if something miraculous was bubbling up.

Snowflake crawled out of her hood and hopped onto the sand. He sniffed the ground and scampered back as the sand moved again.

Kiri leaned closer to get a better look. A black snout, smaller than the tip of her pinkie finger, poked through the sand. Then another snout emerged, and another. Soon there were ten or twenty tiny black snouts, followed by wriggling necks and blinking blue eyes. Thin flippers pushed against the sand as teardrop-shaped bodies squirmed out.

They were turtles! Perfect, miniature versions of the sea turtle Kiri had seen all those weeks before, with ridged shell-like backs and white speckles on their black skin, like stars in the midnight sky.

The turtles kept climbing out of the ground. Once they surfaced, they braced their flippers against the sand and shoved themselves forward in an odd, stutter-stop way. Each one looked exactly like the mother turtle, and yet they were so small—smaller even than the palm of Kiri's hand or the stuffed turtle Ap had given her.

"*Hatchlings,*" whispered Kiri. More turtles crawled out of the sand. "Leatherback hatchlings!"

She looked up, wanting to share this incredible sight with her mother. But her ma wasn't there—not in a way she could see or touch. Still, Kiri knew her mother had led her to this. She thought she'd been called away by a ghost, but instead she'd been called to life. New life.

Kiri's breath caught and her eyes blurred. She hadn't let herself cry for weeks. Not when the sea turtle had been killed, or when she'd been kicked out of the village, or when the panther had been shot. The tears hadn't gone away. They'd simply built up, and now her eyes overflowed with them. They poured down her cheeks in big, warm sobs. She couldn't stop crying. She cried for her mother, and for the panther, and for the incredible miracle of leatherback hatchlings emerging from the sand like tiny fragments of hope.

"I'll stay," she whispered to the shadows before her. "I'll tend the tree. Goodbye, Ma."

# -28-

## The Ocean's Seeds

The turtles paid Snowflake no mind. As soon as they made it to the surface, they set off toward the ocean, flopping and dragging themselves across the sand like little, determined rowboats on land.

Another layer of turtles emerged after the first. Kiri couldn't believe how many there were. She laughed, even while tears trickled down her cheeks.

"So it's started," said a driftwood voice.

Kiri glanced up. The thin, stooped form of the woman who'd presided over nearly every birth in the village stood nearby.

"I check on them in the evenings, when the air turns cool like this," said the Witch Woman. "Something I remember from when I was a girl, younger than you, even, is that turtle hatchlings always emerge when the temperature shifts and night begins."

"*You* did this?" Kiri's thoughts skipped back to the night of the feast, before she'd been marked by the panther. She recalled the white orbs that the Witch Woman had collected in a bucket. They were turtle eggs! That was why the Witch Woman had been close to the sea-grape tunnels when Kiri encountered the panther. She'd been burying the eggs, just like the mother turtle would have done if she hadn't been killed.

"I merely helped nature along," said the Witch Woman. "The real miracle is what you did."

"I didn't do anything," said Kiri. "I didn't save the sea turtle or the panthers, or anything. I failed."

The corners of the Witch Woman's eyes crinkled as her lips turned upward. "No, Kiri. Because of you, things might be different now. What happened before doesn't need to happen again."

Paulo approached. His mouth fell open as he saw the hatchlings. "How did you—"

Before Kiri could explain, Paulo shouted for others to come see. "Look!" he yelled, pointing at several hatchlings flopping across the sand. "Water devi!"

Tae and Akash and some other fugees ran to see what all the fuss was about. Spotting the hatchlings, they called others over until dozens of villagers were rushing across the beach toward them.

Murmurs spread through the crowd. Kiri feared what

the fugees might do. The hatchlings were so small and helpless. What if netters bucketed them to use as bait? Or hungry villagers caught them to cook and eat, like they'd done with the mother sea turtle?

"It's time," said the Witch Woman. "Tell them what to do."

A few of the tiny turtles were going in the wrong direction. Others were stuck behind mounds of trash they couldn't climb over. All around her, Kiri sensed the hatchlings' frantic need to reach the water. The ocean had called to her in a similar way when she'd been stuck in the waller city, but this seemed much stronger and more urgent. The turtles could smell and taste the ocean, and they needed to get to it quickly.

Seagulls circled overhead and crabs peeked out of their holes, looking for a meal, but the people merely stood. Then a crab raced from a hole and tugged at one of the hatchlings. A seagull dove to eat another.

"Help them!" shouted Kiri. "They need to get to the waves!"

To her surprise, the villagers listened. They shooed the seagulls and crabs away, and lifted the fragile tear-shaped bodies over trash and holes, shepherding them to the ocean. There were fifty or sixty hatchlings now, spread across the beach. And for each one, someone from the village stood nearby, making sure the hatchling's path to the water was clear.

Kiri watched, amazed by how gentle people could be with the smallest of beings. Then she spotted Sonia and

Martin near the water's edge. They must have seen all the commotion.

"Get a collection bin!" ordered Sonia, speaking to one of the soldiers back at the tridrone. "Hurry!"

A second soldier stayed with Sonia and Martin, pointing his gun at nearby fugees and shouting at them to keep their distance. The tension between the two groups felt thick and familiar.

Kiri raced to her father, careful not to step on any hatchlings flopping toward the waves.

"I can't believe it!" said Sonia. "*Dermochelys coriacea!* I thought they were extinct. This is incredible! Martin, there's one. Quickly!"

Martin had a plastic collection bin with five or six hatchlings in it. Sonia picked up another hatchling that had almost made it to the water and put it in the bin. Villagers stood, grim-faced, as the wallers captured what they'd tried to release, but none of the fugees dared approach with the soldier standing guard.

"Let them go," said Kiri.

Sonia was too preoccupied with capturing hatchlings to acknowledge her.

Kiri tugged on her father's arm. "Da! Listen. You have to let them go."

"We need to preserve them, Kiribati. They'll die out there. Sharks will eat them, or they'll choke on trash, or get tangled in debris. Catching them is the only way."

"Why won't you listen to me?"

Martin kept collecting hatchlings.

"They belong here," said Kiri. "If you take them, they'll die. Like Ma died."

Her father paused.

The words had slipped out before she'd thought about them. She'd never confronted her da about her mother's death before. Never blamed him for it—not aloud.

For several heartbeats he stared at her with knotted brow. She feared she'd broken something between them and now her da would reject her.

"They belong here," she repeated. "So did Ma. So do I."

Her father's gaze softened. "Are you sure? We could have a good life in the city."

Kiri touched the waller mark on her arm. The city might be part of her, but it wasn't the place for her. "I want to stay here. This is my home."

"It's too dangerous here. Nothing will be easy."

"Nothing worth doing is ever easy, right?" she said, using the phrase he often did. "We can't hide behind walls, waiting for things to get better. We have to change things now. We have to tend the tree."

The words must have sparked something in her father because a look flashed across his face, like he'd found something that he lost long ago. "You . . . sound like your mother," he finally said. "She always talked about protecting the whole tree instead of just a few fallen leaves." His gaze fell to the turtles swimming in the bin he held. Then he took a deep breath and nodded, as if completing a conversation in his head. "Perhaps she was right."

Without another word, Martin pried back the lid of the

collection bin and released all the hatchlings he'd captured into the clear water of a receding wave.

The turtle hatchlings swam into the surf. Some immediately got pulled out by the current, while others were pushed back by incoming waves. Still, they moved much more swiftly in water than they did on land, and one by one they disappeared into the depths of the ocean.

"What are you doing?" demanded Sonia. She splashed through the water to catch a hatchling Martin had released. "Those are all we have. Collect them!"

The soldier turned his gun on Martin.

"Sonia," said Martin. "If there's no place left for them to live, then what's the point?"

"But they're worth—"

"More than we'll ever know," finished Martin.

"I can't believe this. You're giving up?" asked Sonia.

"No. It's the other way around. I'm learning to hope again," said Martin. He walked over to Kiri and put a hand on her shoulder.

"Da?" she asked, wondering if he was okay.

He leaned down and hugged her so tight her feet left the ground.

Kiri hugged him back, holding on to him like she hadn't done since she was a little kid. He slumped but didn't let go. "I should have paid more attention, Kiribati. You grew up when I wasn't looking."

"This is crazy!" interrupted Sonia. "The hatchlings are all swimming away. They'll be lost!"

Martin finally set Kiri down and regarded Sonia. "I don't know how the mother leatherback managed to survive for so long," he said. "Maybe it *was* a miracle, or a devi like some of the fugees claim. What I do know is that sea turtles always return to the beach where they were born to nest. Which means, if some of these hatchlings survive they'll come back here someday to lay their eggs."

"But that could take years," said Sonia. "It could be a decade or two before we even know if any survived."

"It's a big ocean. Some will find a way," said Martin. "And when they do, out of all the beaches in the world, these turtles—the only known leatherbacks in existence—will return here. So if Gen Tech wants to collect leatherback hatchlings, then this beach better be here, and these people better watch over it. Don't you agree?"

Kiri suddenly understood what her father had done by releasing the hatchlings. She turned to Sonia and grabbed her hand. "Sonia, don't be angry. This could be a really good thing."

Gradually the lines in Sonia's brow eased. "If any sea turtles return here," she said. "I know Gen Tech wouldn't want to risk losing such valuable assets. They'd want to make sure they could claim them, and the best way to do that would be to work with the fugees to turn this section of the coast into a refuge."

"And if Gen Tech and the fugees turned this part of the coast into a refuge," added Kiri, "then wouldn't it make sense to bring the panther cubs back here as well?"

"It could. But that's a big risk," said Sonia. "Someone from Gen Tech would need to oversee the project."

Kiri looked to her da. There was a mischievous glint to his eyes that she hadn't seen in years.

"I might know a father and daughter who'd be willing to give it a try," he said.

"Definitely," agreed Kiri, squeezing her father's hand.

Sonia sent the soldiers back to the tridrone, which helped ease the tension with the fugees. No one interfered as the villagers shepherded the remaining hatchlings to the waves. Kiri, Martin, and Sonia stood by the water's edge and watched the last ones swim into the darkening water.

Once all the hatchlings were gone, Martin walked Sonia back to the tridrone to work out the details of what they'd tell the Gen Tech board. Kiri stayed behind with Snowflake. The poor rat had gotten splashed by a wave and was shivering. Every time she stopped petting him, he nudged her hand until she stroked his fur again.

At last, the tridrone thrust pods whirred to life. Kiri waved goodbye to Sonia and wished her luck. Her da came to join her at the ocean's edge. The nearly full moon cast a silvery light across the tops of the waves while the jagged remains of the ruins offshore looked blacker than black, like pieces cut out of existence.

"It's not going to be easy," said her da. "Trying to

change the way people live never is. If this has any chance of working, from now on everyone in the village will need to be a protector of the Shadow That Hunts."

"We'll be more than that," said Kiri. "You'll see. We'll be much, much more."

# Epilogue

Kiri and her da arranged their picnic blanket between two dunes near where the hatchlings had emerged almost eight weeks before.

Several other families had set up picnics along the edge of the sea grapes and ghost forest as well. Kiri saw Paulo, Tae, and Charro's blanket a little ways down the beach. And Nessa, Senek, and Akash were just beyond them. Some families had brought small tables, and they set out plates and cups of offerings on them, while others had hung strings of flowers and brightly painted bones from twisty sea grape branches. Everyone in the village had lost someone, but today wasn't a sad day. Instead, people were in a festive mood. They ate, drank, and played, setting out extra cups and sweets for those not there.

It was Kiri's first celebration of the dead. Martin had been reluctant to make much of a fuss about it, but since their stilt house had been airlifted to the village almost two months ago, he'd been willing to go along with the village's traditions. And besides, he couldn't get much work done today—not with all the aqua farmers, caretakers, and rangers he'd been training taking the day off. So once the panther cubs were fed and cared for, he'd come back to the beach to picnic with Kiri.

Kiri arranged the food she'd made, or had tried to make, on their blanket. The jellyfish soup was runny, and the seaweed-clam-and-coconut skewers had gotten burned. Cooking wasn't her specialty, but Paulo and the Witch Woman had been trying to teach her how to make a few simple dishes. And everyone in the village was learning to cook some of the new foods they had now, like the seaweed and clams they'd begun to farm. Raising edible seaweed had been Kiri's idea. The first harvests were already coming in, and the spicy soup Paulo made with it tasted delicious.

Like most fugees, Kiri put out an extra plate of food for the dead—just one plate for both her ma and the panther since the two felt connected. Maybe their spirits were the same. She didn't really expect the ghost of her mother or the panther to show up and eat the food. Still, she wanted to do something to remember them. So she set out the plate along with an extra cup of water sweetened with honey-suckle blossoms.

Her father raised an eyebrow at the food for ghosts,

but he made no comment about it. Instead, they talked about Skitter, Mustache, and Cricket, and all the ridiculous things the cubs had done recently. They were growing and developing new behaviors so quickly it was hard to keep up. Already, in the weeks since the cubs had been brought back, they'd had to expand the cubs' enclosure twice, and Martin had plans to make it even bigger still.

The long-term plan, though, was to get rid of the fence entirely. Once the cubs were big enough to roam on their own, Martin planned on using a network of small drones and cameras to keep track of the panthers and make sure they were safe. That way they could expand the cubs' territory and breed them with samples from similar subspecies.

"Sonia thinks that if this collaboration continues to go well, Gen Tech might use it as a model for how to create other wildlife refuges," said Martin.

"Meaning what, exactly?" asked Kiri.

"Meaning we might have visitors soon, so we better clean our house."

"Our house *is* clean."

"Last I counted, Snowflake had four nests in the sleeping loft. And one of them was made of shredded paper from my books."

"That's because Snowflake loves to read," said Kiri.

Her da smirked. "Speaking of which, Sonia tells me you need to catch up on your homeschool work."

"Snowflake ate my homeschool work."

"Nice try," replied her da. "Rats don't eat vid screens."

As if to prove Martin's point, Snowflake snatched a

honeysuckle blossom from the bowl Kiri had set out and daintily chewed on one end.

Kiri considered shooing him away from the food for ghosts, but she decided not to. "Go on, Snowflake. Best not to waste food," she said.

Snowflake finished the honeysuckle blossom and sniffed a coconut-and-clam skewer. Then he tore into it hungrily.

Kiri didn't mind that she hadn't seen her mother or felt her presence since the day the turtles had hatched. Maybe it meant her mother was happy and able to move on. Or maybe, Kiri thought, it meant *she* was happy and able to move on. Of course she still missed her mother, but she no longer felt that part of herself was missing.

During the day she worked with her da, training fugees and restoring parts of the coast. And at night she had homeschool work to do. Fortunately, Ap had been helping her catch up on reading and math through chat sessions every night. Sometimes he even made her funny vids to demonstrate things.

Thinking of Ap, Kiri reached into her pocket and touched the stuffed turtle he'd given her. He'd told her it would bring her luck, and it had. Every time she thought what they were doing here was crazy or pointless, she reached into her pocket and squeezed the turtle. The little stuffed animal reminded her of the hatchlings, and it reminded her that restoring this part of the coast wasn't just about turtles and panthers. It was about people, too. People like Ap, who'd never seen the ocean but were still connected to it in countless ways.

"I almost forgot," said her da, startling Kiri from her thoughts. "Sonia sent something for you in the last supply tridrone."

"What is it?" asked Kiri, hoping it wasn't more home-school work.

"Beats me." Her da pulled a small box from his pack.

The box was wrapped in brown paper with the words *For the bravest protector I know* written on the outside.

Kiri was careful not to rip the paper as she opened it. Paper like this was a luxury, and she could make dozens of things out of it. She lifted the cover to the box and found a knife with a shiny fixed blade and an elegant bamboo handle.

Kiri held the knife. Sunlight glinted off the polished blade.

"What do you think?" asked her da.

"You told her to give me this?"

"She wanted to give you something, and I knew you needed one," he said. "Be careful. It's sharper than your ma's was."

Kiri picked up a piece of palm wood and started carving it to test the blade. Before she knew it, she was shaping the wood into a small round disk. Then she began to add a head and fins, and ridges to the back. The more she added, the more she remembered about the leatherback hatchlings.

Paulo and Tae and a few other kids must have seen her new knife shimmering in the sunlight, because they came over and asked what she was doing.

"I'm carving a hatchling," she said. "It's a tradition."

"No it isn't," said Tae.

"It will be for me," she said.

Paulo and Tae looked at each other. They each got out their own knives and started to carve little leatherback hatchlings as well. Word spread, and before long other kids were carving them, too. The youngest asked their parents to carve leatherback hatchlings for them. Soon several adults were creating their own tiny reminders of the sea turtles.

Kiri took great care to give her hatchling every detail she could recall, from the ridges on the back to the small triangular tail to the four thin flippers and wrinkled skin. When she was done, she colored her carving black with charcoal from one of the fire pits and used crushed pieces of shell to give it white speckles. Finally, she added two small pieces of blue sea glass for the eyes.

It was nearly sunset by the time she finished. She walked to the ocean's edge with the hatchling she'd carved. Paulo and Tae came with her, bringing their own hatchling carvings, along with Charro and her da. Most of the village stood near the shore, and almost every family had carved at least one sea turtle.

They seemed to be waiting for her to start. She didn't know what to say, so she simply walked to the water and set her turtle on the lip of a receding wave. Others did the same, placing their hatchlings on the waves in silence.

Dozens of carved turtles floated back and forth while the villagers watched. They looked tiny and fragile. Doubt filled Kiri as she gazed out at the crushing waves and the ruins beyond them. There were so many possibilities for disaster, it seemed ludicrous to think that any of the real hatchlings could survive and grow, and one day return to this beach to nest.

A few of the wooden hatchlings got stranded on the beach or hung up on debris. Kids immediately ran to them and carried them back to the water, giggling and shouting as if they were real turtles.

A smile crept onto Kiri's face. Even if none of the sea turtles came back, the fugees would at least be able to say that they'd done what they could. They'd tried to protect the land and water, and that made them part of things in a way they hadn't been before.

Amid all the waves and chaos, Kiri's attention shifted to one wooden hatchling. It looked like the one she'd carved. The palm wood must have gotten waterlogged, because the hatchling no longer floated. Instead, it bobbed beneath the crest of an oncoming wave, and its blue eyes sparkled.

Perhaps it was only a trick of the light through the rippling water, or an illusion caused by the current. For a moment, though, the carved turtle's flippers appeared to move, as if the hatchling was swimming off. It dove deeper into the next wave, vanishing into the darkness like an ocean's seed being planted. A dream from a world long gone. A shimmering fragment of hope. A tiny, fragile shard of what could be again.

# Author's Note

On the day I completed this book, scientists estimated that fewer than 180 Florida panthers currently existed in the wild. They are one of the most critically endangered subspecies in North America.

Leatherback sea turtles, one of the largest reptiles on earth, are also critically endangered, as are many types of gorillas, tigers, rhinos, elephants, dolphins, whales, and countless other species.

According to scientists, if present trends continue, by the end of this century half of all plant and animal species will be extinct or on the edge of extinction. Among the main causes of extinction are habitat loss, poaching, and climate change.

It doesn't have to be this way. Many people are working to save species from extinction and to protect vital habitats so that we can all live in a more abundant, sustainable, wonder-filled world. You can join them.

To learn more about easy actions you can take and organizations you can join, visit ToddMitchellBooks.com.

# Acknowledgments

*And I saw the sacred hoop of my people was*
*one of many hoops that made one circle, wide*
*as daylight and as starlight, and in the center*
*grew one mighty flowering tree to shelter all the*
*children of one mother and one father.*

—BLACK ELK, FROM *BLACK ELK SPEAKS*

This book wouldn't exist without the help, support, and love of a whole stilt-village full of inspiring people. It's impossible to name them all, but I want to give a special shout-out to my extraordinarily perceptive editor, Kate Sullivan, and to the amazing team at Delacorte Press for helping this become the book it is. Kate, you made this a labor of love for yourself as well as for me, and for that I'm deeply grateful.

A shimmering net full of thanks goes out to all the readers who patiently read early versions of this book, especially Laura Resau, Sharman Russell, Leah Colasuonno, Kerri Mitchell (whom I made cry a little!), and my daughter, Addison Story, who gave me both inspiration and excellent advice. Plus, she named Snowflake.

A skiff full of thanks goes out to my incredible agent, Ginger Knowlton, for believing in me all these years, and for being a wise voice of sanity in this crazy business. And many thanks to the excellent folks at Curtis Brown, Ltd., for putting up with my endless questions.

Thank you to my family, my parents, and my parents-in-law for giving me writing retreats to escape to. Most of all, I'm deeply grateful to my wife, Kerri, for taking this journey with me. I know living with a writer is rarely easy, K, but you do it with grace and style. You're the person I most want to share stories with at the end of the day.

To my daughters, Addison Story and Cailin Elizabeth, thank you for giving me the two best reasons to write for young readers that I've ever had.

To all the readers (yes, you, holding this book right now!), teachers, and librarians who've read my books and invited me to speak over the years—you've given me a way to pursue my dreams, and for that I'm immensely grateful. And thank you to the many brave souls, especially the young ones, who are working right now to protect the wonder of the natural world. You give me hope.

Finally, I owe much gratitude to Black Elk for sharing his visions over a hundred years ago and, by doing so, helping me and many others see the tree in the center of the circle that connects us all.

# About the Author

TODD MITCHELL is the author of the middle-grade novel *The Traitor King* and the young adult novels *The Secret to Lying* and *Backwards*. He has never caught a panther, but he has worked to rescue wolves, rehabilitated injured hawks, taken care of orphaned bear cubs, and built homes for foxes. He teaches creative writing at Colorado State University in Fort Collins, where he lives with his wife, two spirited and creative daughters, and one very smart dog. You can visit him (and arrange to bring him to your school) at ToddMitchellBooks.com.